BARRY PAIN'S
PUZZLE STORIES

BARRY PAIN'S
PUZZLE STORIES

Detection Without Crime
The Problem Club

COACHWHIP PUBLICATIONS

Greenville, Ohio

Barry Pain's Puzzle Stories
Barry Pain (1864-1928)
"Detection Without Crime" stories, collected 1915 (*One Kind and Another*).
The Problem Club, first published 1917-18, collected 1919.
© 2013 Coachwhip Publications
No claims made on public domain material.
Cover and title page images from *Strand Magazine* (Problem Club stories).

CoachwhipBooks.com

ISBN 1-61646-173-X
ISBN-13 978-1-61646-173-7

CONTENTS

DETECTION WITHOUT CRIME

From the Note-Book
of the Late Horace Fish

On Green Paper

Most of my friends are acquainted with my hobby—a solution of those mysteries which are to be found in everyday life. Some of them put this differently, and say that I have a disgusting tendency to poke my curious nose into other people's affairs. Some make fun of me. I am not in the least affected either by their ridicule or their condemnation. I am an old man, and one of the few gifts of old age is independent judgment. I have indeed been pleased to find a hobby which provides me with some occupation. It may be that in some cases I have shown a certain amount of ingenuity in obtaining the correct solution of what at first sight seemed extremely puzzling: indeed my worst enemies would admit that this is so. It is also my belief that if they came upon anything which bothered and mystified them, they would bring it to me and see what I could make of it.

The Reverend Septimus Erde has never ridiculed me. He has never ridiculed anybody or anything. He has a serious profession, and he is by nature a very serious man. I am told that his views are slightly narrow and fanatical, but that is a point upon which I am in no position to speak. I have known Erde for many years, and I knew his father before him. When at eleven o'clock one morning my servant told me that Mr. Erde wished to see me, I did not at once connect it with my peculiar hobby. To tell the truth, I thought he had probably called for a subscription—a thing that he has done before, perhaps too frequently. I therefore crossed the passage into the drawing-room in rather an irritated frame of mind. And when

I asked Mr. Erde what I could do for him, it was without the slight-est intention of doing it. He is not a bad-looking young man, obvi-ously sincere and straightforward.

"I have called, Mr. Fish," he said, "to ask for your kind assis-tance."

"Alas," I said. "I have so many calls upon me nowadays, that—"

"You misunderstand me. It is true that many charitable enter-prises in which I am interested are at present crippled from want of funds, but I had not intended this morning to make any further demands on your generosity in that respect. The fact of the case is that I have come upon a problem which has a peculiar interest for me. You perhaps can help me to solve it."

This put an entirely different complexion on matters. I was ready and even eager to hear what he had to say.

"For the last few days I have been staying at Aldeburgh. I have been overworked lately, and my medical man strongly advised a short rest and change. Yesterday morning I strolled out beyond the town. A fresh wind was blowing, and a torn scrap of green pa-per was blown along to my feet. Some words on it caught my eye, and I picked it up. Here it is."

He produced from his note-book a scrap of green note-paper. The words written on it were: "You must take the veil."

It was easy to see that it was the handwriting of a man, and moreover of an educated man.

"Well," I said. "And what else did you find?"

"I was returning to town that day, and I had very little time before me. I could only find one other scrap of the green paper, and that was some yards away in a furze bush."

He produced it and handed it to me. The second scrap ran: "Disregarding their anger entirely."

"Now, Mr. Fish," said Erde, "I need not insult your intelligence by telling you what this means. Some poor girl is being forced into the convent life, contrary to the wishes of her parents, who are naturally angry about it. It is amazing that these things should happen at the present day, but we know they do happen. I feel it to be my duty to prevent this, if possible. But I do not know the name of the girl or the priest who wrote that letter. I do not know where she lives. Can you help me to find out these things, Mr. Fish? For once you have a chance of turning your undoubted abilities to real account."

"I will see what can be done," I said, and rang the bell. In reply to my enquiries I found that the wind on the previous day had been from the north-east, and was still blowing from the same quarter.

"That at any rate is satisfactory," I said.

"Why?" asked Mr. Erde

"Because any other scraps of this letter will have been carried inland, and not out to sea. As they are carried inland, they are probably recoverable. It is only a question of a little time and patience. I shall go down to Aldeburgh at once, and within a week I have no doubt that I shall be able to give you information upon which you can act."

Erde had done one very sensible thing. He had made a careful and exact note of the point at which he had found those two scraps of green paper, and had also drawn a rough plan.

"You really mean," he said, "that you will go down to Aldeburgh and stay there perhaps for days, simply in order to help a poor deluded girl, whose very name you do not know? It does you great credit, Mr. Fish."

"I'm afraid," I said, "that I must put it that I am going down there in order to solve a mystery which fascinates me. My time hangs heavily on my hands, Mr. Erde, and I can assure you that I am very much obliged to you for having provided me with my favourite occupation."

On arriving at Aldeburgh late that afternoon, I left my luggage at the hotel, engaged a room there, and proceeded at once to the point which Mr. Erde had indicated. I found his plan of great use. I could see no scrap of green paper anywhere, but I found something else, which I thought might be of use to me—a boy scout diligently engaged in making a sketch map.

"Hullo," I said. "Are you a scout?"

"Yes, sir," said the boy distrustfully. The distrust was natural. There was no obvious reason why I should have spoken to him.

"Oh," I said. "I have heard about you boy scouts. You are supposed to keep your eyes peeled, aren't you? to keep a sharp lookout for things."

He admitted grudgingly that this was part of the idea.

"Well now," I said, "just for fun let me give you a little test. When did you last see some scraps of green paper?"

"Just about where I am now, on the day before yesterday at three in the afternoon."

"That's right," I said. "You're a smart boy. Now then, as a test for memory, what did you find written on those scraps of paper?"

"It was a letter torn up. I don't want to read other people's letters, do I?"

That was rather awkward. "Certainly not," I said. "No more do I. But this is an exceptional case. On the recovery of those scraps of green paper depends in all probability the safety or ruin of a girl."

"I don't like sells," said the boy.

"It is quite natural that you should think it a sell, but it is not. I am acting in this case for a clergyman, the Reverend Septimus Erde. Here is his card. Here is a rough plan showing exactly where those scraps of paper were to be found. I cannot tell you anything more, but I have shown you enough to show you that the thing is genuine."

"Let's have a look at the plan," said the boy. He looked at it carefully. "Yes," he said, "that's right. If those scraps of paper are to be found, I'll get them for you."

"Good boy," I said. "Now the direction of the wind—"

"Oh, I know all about that. I shall allow for that. It has been dry weather, and the grass is short. Those scraps of paper may have gone a long way. Still, I'll do what I can. Where shall I bring them?"

I gave him my name and told him at which hotel I was staying. "I shall be there for two or three days."

"I can't be here to-morrow morning," said the boy. "But I'll have a look now, and another look to-morrow afternoon. Then if I have not got it, I'll give up."

"Don't give up, my boy," I said. "Try, try, try again. You remember Bruce of Scotland."

"Yes," said the boy. "But I've got lots of other things to do. If I can't find them, there's nothing to stop you going on trying yourself, is there?"

His manner was outwardly polite, but he was a disconcerting boy. However, I felt that he was on his mettle. I had aroused the tracking instinct in him. I felt sure that if he could find any scrap of that letter on green paper, he would bring it to me in triumph.

The next morning I took a look on my own account, and found nothing. In the evening, just after I had finished dinner, I was told that a boy wished to see me. I found my young friend in the hall.

"I've found three bits of the green paper, sir," said the boy. "They were three hundred and forty-one yards away from the place where you were looking, and not in the direction you would have thought the wind would have taken them. The wind is a queer thing on broken ground like that. There are eddies and back currents, and—"

"Yes," I said, "quite so. Let's have a look."

He handed me the scraps of paper one by one. On the first were the words: "You must depend," which fitted in with what had gone before, but gave no further information. The second scrap was very small, and contained only two words: "The smoke." The use of incense at once occurred to my mind. The third scrap was larger and contained one short sentence. For nearly a minute I read it over and over, and then light broke in on me. Somewhat to the boy's astonishment I burst out laughing.

"That's all right," I said. "You need not hunt for any more. The mystery is cleared up." I gave him gingerbeer, which he accepted gladly, and while he was drinking it I told him the whole story. I then gave him half a sovereign, which he accepted reluctantly, saying that he had not done the thing for money.

"No," I said. "But what you have found is worth a good deal more than half a sovereign to me, it gives me that feeling of solid satisfaction which is almost priceless."

I telegraphed to Erde to meet my train next morning, and told him that the mystery was solved. I found him, pacing the platform in a state of great perturbation.

"Now then, Mr. Fish," he said. "First and foremost give me the name of the girl."

"There is no girl in the case at all."

"There must be. You have forgotten the reference to the veil, you know."

"Not in the least. I have found three scraps of paper, and I will show you the first two." I did so.

"I must say," he said, "they only tend to confirm one's suspicions. Look at that repeated use of the word 'must.' The girl must disregard the anger of her parents. She must depend entirely upon the priest. Those words 'the smoke' refer clearly to a part of the Romish ceremony. Let me see the third scrap."

"Wait a minute, Mr. Erde. I'm going to tell you a story. There was a man once who took a house where there was a bee-hive. In course of time he wished to take the honey, but he did not know how to set about it. He therefore wrote to a friend who had experience of these matters. The friend replied that he must take the lid off the hive, disregarding the anger of the bees, and that he must then take the veil and wrap it carefully round his head. He must depend, however, far more on the smoke, provided, as you know, by a little bellows arrangement that the bee-keeper uses. If you want further proof, here is the third scrap, on which is written: 'Tie your trousers tightly round the ankles with a bit of string.' A very excellent precaution if you do not want your legs stung."

"You are a wonderful man, Mr. Fish," said Erde. But I could not help thinking that he looked rather disappointed.

The Face of the Corpse

I was sitting in the club one morning, working out the solution of a cypher advertisement, when old Paget, looking like a discontented chimpanzee, came shuffling up to me.

"Mornin'," he said. "You're always a good deal interested in other people's business, Fish, ain't you?"

"Not always. Seldom, in fact. Only when it happens to be interesting—"

"Well, I've got something in your line. I had a chat with Brook, my solicitor, yesterday—wanting to know about a fellow that's taking a house of mine. Brook said he'd make an inquiry and let me know on the telephone. Sure enough, soon after I got home, I was rung up. Voice that I took to be my solicitor's said: 'I've made that inquiry for you.' So I said: 'Thanks very much. What's the result?' And then came the extraordinary thing, Fish. The same voice went on: 'The face of the corpse has turned a pinkish colour—much the same as in life.'"

"Yes," I said. "That promises fairly well. And you led him on, I hope."

"Sorry to say I didn't. Thing staggered me. I asked what on earth he was talking about. Then he wanted to know to whom he was speaking, and I told him. 'Sorry,' says the fellow. 'Wrong number,' and cut himself off."

"I see," I said. "And did you ask the Exchange who had rung you up?"

"Well," said old Paget, "I didn't think of it at the moment. Doubt if they could have told me. Besides, it might have been somebody speaking from a public call-office. All I know is that it wasn't my solicitor."

"There's nothing to go on," I said.

"Nothing whatever that I can see. Thought it would fox you. Lots of things happening every day, Fish, that you'll never be able to explain. Tragedy somewhere though—you may depend on it." And he moved away, shaking his head solemnly.

Not being a detective in a story-book, my methods are so simple as to be almost childish. When I don't know, I ask—a thing apparently that no good detective would ever stoop to. On this occasion there was my authority ready to hand. Dr. Boden was sitting in one corner of the room, reading the *Times*. He is a dapper little man, with an eyeglass, able enough but a little too superior for my taste.

I went over to him and said, with an apology for the queerness of the question: "I wonder, doctor, if you could tell me why the face of a corpse turned pink."

"It didn't," said Dr. Boden. "It couldn't. The thing's a physiological impossibility. The face might change colour somewhat from decomposition, but certainly it would not turn pink. Somebody's been having a game with you, Mr. Fish."

I knew better. Old Paget is a solid, dreary man, without one spark of humour in him. Compared with Paget, Bradshaw's time-tables are fanciful. There was the possibility that somebody had been having a game with old Paget, but I did not think it at all likely; in that case the joke would have been carried further and there would have been more details.

So I felt as if I had gone down a blind alley and bumped my head against the wall at the further end. For the time I put old Paget's problem aside, and went back to the advertisement in cypher. The cyphers used in what is sometimes called the agony column, have not as a rule been invented by experts, and are quite easy to read for anyone who has studied the subject. It may be added that they are seldom worth reading. They consist generally of the ecstatic rubbish of separated lovers. It took me ten minutes to read the advertisement on which I was engaged. I transcribed it as follows, in my note-book:

"Thousand from H.-L. Joy. Give month's notice, and rejoin the squatter of Mardel. Boys must try cycling again."

It seemed that the advertiser had received a thousand pounds, and in consequence somebody was to give up present employment—presumably, from the length of notice, of a menial character—and rejoin a person described as the squatter of Mardel, who might perhaps be the advertiser. But what boys were to begin cycling, and why? I could make nothing of it, and I went back to old Paget's problem. As I turned it over in my mind, I thought I saw now a faint gleam of hope. I could not find out who it was that had unintentionally rung Paget up, but there was just a possibility that I might discover the man for whose telephone number Paget's had been mistaken. The figures of Paget's number were 1409. Five and nine have a slight similarity of sound, and if the mistake had been made in the Exchange, it was possible that the man who had been given 1409 had really asked for 1405. I determined to take the chance of it, at any rate, and to find out who was the holder of 1405 at that Exchange.

I rang up 1405 and began speaking as if I had been a business firm: "We find that your order was despatched this morning, and you should have received it by now."

A weary voice answered me: "Who's speaking?"

"Lancing and Co., Victoria Street," I said glibly, taking the first name and address that occurred to my imagination.

"Don't remember order."

"Surely," I said. "To whom are we speaking?"

"To the secretary of the late Mr. Holmes-Larrival."

"Indeed? Then I fear we have the wrong number. So sorry to have troubled you." I hung up the receiver. I found from the directory that 1405 was the number for Holmes-Larrival's private address, not for his business office. I knew something of the man, for he had died but three days before, and I had read his obituary notice. He was a millionaire, an Australian by birth who had been settled in this country for the last twenty years. That obituary notice had come as near to an unfavourable criticism as it very well could. "Strong in his domestic affections, but merciless in his business dealings," was a phrase that came back to my mind. There had been a reference, too, to his eccentricity.

Now Holmes-Larrival died in his bed in his own house. Therefore a message relating to the colour of the dead man's face might conceivably have been sent *from* his address, but could hardly have been sent *to* it. This bothered me.

On the other hand it looked to me as if in searching for one thing I had stumbled on another. I had been reminded of Holmes-Larrival, and it seemed likely that the cypher advertisement referred to him. There were his initials. The thousand would be a legacy. It is true the legacies are not generally announced on the day following the death of the testator, but in this case there might have been some special reason. The word "squatter" is specially Australian, and Holmes-Larrival was of Australian origin. Probably the advertiser had been a friend of the dead man in his youth; and this would account for the legacy. Following where the light led me, I looked up Mardel in the big atlas in the reading-room. I could find no place of that name, but I did find that there was a village called Mardel Boys within twenty miles of London—Boys being an obvious corruption of the French *bois*. Here was another step. It showed me that I had transcribed that advertisement wrongly. It should have run: "Rejoin the squatter of Mardel Boys. Must try cycling again." I now determined to go to Mardel Boys, and to continue my investigations there. I ordered sandwiches, a whisky and soda, and the ABC. I lunched hurriedly, and by three that afternoon I was in Mardel Boys.

Mardel Boys must at one time have been as picturesque a village as you would find in Hertfordshire. It is still quite charming, but it is waking up and the builder is busy there. I sought out the house-agent; house-agents have always a large fund of information, and are willing to impart it—the sunnier part of it at least—to prospective tenants or purchasers. I told the agent that I was Mr. C. N. M. Buckley, and that I was anxious to purchase a little place in the neighbourhood. I wanted a good house and a matured garden, and I did not wish to go beyond twelve thousand. I must admit that the only one of these statements which was at all true was that I did not wish to go beyond twelve thousand.

I went very thoroughly into the question of the house itself. Then I had something to say about other points. The services at the parish church were not too ritualistic, I hoped. Were the residents desirable from the social point of view? I had heard of an Australian who had settled there—for the moment the name had escaped my memory.

The agent thought very hard, but he could not remember any Australian living in the locality. This was disappointing, though he hastened to assure me that there were quite a number of residents who were up to the motor-car standard. But I persevered. Was the local doctor satisfactory?

"Oh, yes, sir," said the agent. "A very clever man—Dr. Cogswell. He's attended me and my family many a year."

"I should have thought there was room for a second man in a growing place like this."

"Well, as a matter of fact we have a second man—Dr. Orbright, fully qualified. He came and squatted here about two years ago. A very pleasant gentleman, I believe; but, of course, he has very little practice so far."

At the word "squatted" I pricked up my ears. "Squatted?" I said. "What does that mean?"

"Well, sir, that's a word I had from Dr. Cogswell. It seems that in the medical professional, when a doctor comes to a place and does not buy a practice, but just puts up his plate and takes his chance, then he is known as a squatter."

"I see," I said. And after that my interview with the house-agent very soon came to an end. I felt that I had struck the right track. Dr. Orbright then was "the squatter of Mardel Boys," and it was to Dr. Orbright that I next went.

Dr. Orbright lived in a tiny house in a newly erected row. The house was well enough kept, but it was rather poorly and sparsely furnished, and did not suggest opulence. The doctor was a very cheery young man of twenty-six. There was no assumption of professional dignity about him. I explained that I was Mr. C. N. M. Buckley, and that as a prospective resident in the neighbourhood I wished to know something of its sanitary character. It was a point, I said, on which I would sooner trust a doctor than a house-agent.

He said he would be very happy to tell me anything he could. So he went into questions of soil and subsoil, water-supply, drainage systems, and the death-rate. I displayed the greatest interest in these subjects, and bored myself profoundly. The doctor accepted my proffered guinea under protest, saying it would never have occurred to him to make a charge for that kind of thing.

"Then, doctor," I said, "I'm afraid you'll never be a millionaire like your friend Holmes-Larrival." The young man looked surprised. "My friend?" he said. "I can assure you I always regarded Holmes-Larrival as my enemy."

"You attended him, I think."

"I attended Holmes-Larrival only once," said Dr. Orbright. "And that was the day after his death."

It was my turn to be surprised. "I don't understand," I said.

"No? I dare say it sounds queer, but it is the case. Yesterday for the first time I attended Holmes-Larrival professionally, and he died the day before."

As he offered no explanation, I thought I would push the thing a little further. "Well," I said, "stranger though I am to you, I hope you will at any rate let me congratulate you on the nice little legacy you receive from your dead patient."

"Thank you," he said, and I fancy he was beginning to be rather annoyed. "You might possibly have heard of a connection between Holmes-Larrival and myself from local gossip, but I do not see how you come to know about the legacy. Holmes-Larrival's solicitors, carrying out his instructions, told me of it, but I have mentioned it to nobody."

"Pardon me," I said. "You advertised it in a newspaper this morning."

"But that was a cypher advertisement. I should have thought it impossible for anyone to read it without the key—"

"As a man who has made some study of cyphers, I must tell you that your own production was so easy as to be almost childish."

"At any rate," he said, "it was no business of yours. It was a private message to my wife."

"My dear sir," I said, "nothing is any business of mine. I have no business. If you want to send a private message to your wife, it would cost you less and the privacy would be better secured, if you used the penny post."

"I had my own reasons. However, I know now how you have found out everything. There's nothing more to be said."

"But I have found out practically nothing. I do not know why somebody has to try cycling again."

"Nor am I going to tell you," said the doctor angrily.

"Nor do I know why the face of the dead man turned pink."

"That was not mentioned in the advertisement. How you come to know anything about that beats me altogether. But you may be quite certain you will learn nothing about it from me. May I suggest that perhaps you have a train to catch?"

This was really rather rude of him. However, I had a screw to turn, and I now proceeded to turn it. "Certainly you may. Good-bye, doctor. I won't fail to send you my little book on newspaper cyphers when it comes out, in gratitude for your interesting contribution to it."

That did it. Before I left, I had promised that his advertisement should not appear in my book, which, by the way, I had never had any intention of writing, and Dr. Orbright had explained everything to me. And when I got the explanation, it was all so simple and obvious that I could have kicked myself for never having thought of it. I got back to town by six, dressed, and returned to the club to dine. I found old Paget discussing with Dr. Boden the future of the Empire—as to which they did not appear to be hopeful.

"Boden and I dining here," said Paget gloomily. "Care to join us?"

I said, of course, that I should be charmed. It was half-way through dinner that Paget mentioned the incident of the morning.

"Fish is fond of ferreting out things," he said to Boden. "But this morning I foxed him. An astonishing thing it was—and, as Fish had to admit, nothing whatever to go on." He told Boden about the telephone message.

"Yes, Paget," I said, "I was quite wrong. As soon as I came to think it over, I saw that there was plenty to go on. I've got the whole thing explained now, though Boden here did mislead me at the start."

"How?" said Boden sharply, putting up his eyeglass

"You told me that the face of a corpse could not be turned pink."

"I did not," snapped Boden. "I told you the face of a corpse could not turn pink—a vastly different thing. The one implies natural process, and the other artificial intervention. Left to itself the face of a corpse could not turn pink. But I am not imbecile enough to tell you or anybody else that a surface cannot be painted. I have myself been asked to rouge the face of a corpse; I refused."

"Well," said Paget, "don't get so quarrelsome. I want the story. Go on, Fish."

"Pure theory, of course," said Boden.

"No theory at all," I said. "It's a simple record of facts—rather long and dull, I am afraid. About a year and a half ago Dr. Orbright, a young practitioner living at Mardel Boys in Hertfordshire, was out bicycling. At a right-angled corner another bicyclist, who was on the wrong side of the road, ran into him. The doctor had one hand a good deal cut about, and his machine was badly damaged. The other bicyclist, who turned out to be the Australian million-aire, Holmes-Larrival, got off scot-free. The doctor put in a mod-erate claim for the damage to his machine, and Holmes-Larrival refused to pay a penny of it. He admitted that he was on the wrong side of the road at the corner, but said that the doctor was equally in the wrong for not ringing his bell. He also intimated that if the claim was pressed he should fight it, and should make it a deuc-edly expensive business for the doctor. Now, the doctor was a poor man. He had started practice in Mardel Boys speculatively. He had recently married. He could not afford to fight a millionaire, and he dropped the claim. You can hardly blame him. He had not even enough to buy himself another bicycle; and the girl he had married had to go out and earn money as a companion. Holmes-Larrival died three days ago. As soon as he was dead, his solicitor went out to Mardel Boys and saw Dr. Orbright, in accordance with instructions he had had from his client. The doctor was told that Holmes-Larrival was to be buried in his native country. It was therefore necessary that his body should be embalmed or preserved, and by the terms of his will Dr. Orbright was to be asked to undertake this work. The will said that the testator hoped that the doctor would show as much zeal in preserving his body as he had on a former occasion in attempting to destroy it. His first impulse was to refuse; then he reflected that he had not so much work that he could afford to throw any away, especially as there would probably be a good fee hanging to it. It was just as well for him that he did, for Holmes-Larrival had left him a legacy of a thousand pounds conditional on that acceptance, a fact that was not to be disclosed to him until he had either accepted or refused."

"Seems to have been a nasty-natured man, this Holmes-thingamy," said old Paget.

"Fairly so. Well, Orbright went up to town next morning to the undertaker's, where the body had been removed for the purpose, and did what was necessary. I believe it's a simple matter nowadays, isn't it, Boden?"

"Oh, yes. They open the radial artery, tie in a vulcanite tube, and inject a solution of formalin. It is generally slightly coloured with carmine, and would have the effect about which you asked me."

"Not often wanted, I should think," said Paget.

"Frequently," said Boden. "Most of the principal undertakers have a man who can do it."

"Well," I said, "the rest of the story is obvious. Mrs. Holmes-Larrival was anxious that there should be no defacement of the corpse, and inquired as to that through the secretary. He rang up the solicitors. They inquired of Orbright, and telephoned the information—as they thought to the secretary. But a mistake was made in the Exchange, and they got 1409, which is Paget's number, instead of 1405, which was Holmes-Larrival's—"

I said nothing about the cypher advertisement. I did not want them to know what a very simple business it had really been. It pleased me to see even Dr. Boden utterly at a loss to say how I had got at the facts.

But a word of further explanation about that advertisement may be given here. Mrs. Orbright had taken a place as companion to an eccentric old lady, a Mrs. Axmund, whose house stood on the top of a Herefordshire hill and was six miles from the nearest village. By arrangement with a railway company, and also with a boy with a bicycle, Mrs. Axmund managed to get the London morning papers on her breakfast table, three hours before the only post in the day reached her house. By using an advertisement in the paper, Dr. Orbright gained time in conveying his good news. It appeared that there were objections to the sending of a telegram. There would be porterage to pay. Mrs. Axmund always insisted on paying this herself, always grumbled at it, and always expected to be shown the telegram in order that she might demonstrate that it need never have been sent. The joking reference to the cycling explains itself.

The Lady of the Pillar-Box

Travelling one day on a Tube railway, I happened to find myself seated opposite to a well-dressed lady of middle age. Her expression was one of timidity and benevolence, and I judged her to be of low mental calibre. The nose was Roman, the forehead receded, and the chin was lamentable. The eyes showed nervousness.

In one hand this lady held a small box wrapped in paper. On one side of the box were the words "DEATH TO ALL," printed in black capitals. I noticed that she was wearing one black shoe and one of bronze green.

These points interested me. I had intended to travel as far as Edgware Road, but when the lady got out at Baker Street, I followed her. On reaching the lift she increased my interest and my perplexity. She said plaintively to the lift-man who took her ticket: "Do you still refuse?"

The man looked slightly sheepish. "Yessum," he said. "I shouldn't know what to do with 'em."

"I suppose it hasn't been found?" she said, after a pause.

"Not that I know of," said the man. "But it wouldn't be—that kind of thing never is. Afraid you had your journey for nothing too."

"Yes," said the lady wearily, "the tree turned out to be a sycamore."

The man smiled and said "Good morning" as he swung the gates open. The lady was too cryptic to be lost sight of, and I followed her down the street.

She went straight to the nearest pillar-box and dropped into it the small box which she was carrying. Then she went off as fast as she could walk. Now, I had observed that box carefully. It bore no stamp and no address—no inscription of any kind except that mysterious "DEATH TO ALL."

Women are universally suspicious of those who ask favours of them. But many of them submit readily to dictation, and it had struck me that this lady was of the number. If I had besought her, with many apologies, to give me the solution of the problem, and spare me nights of sleepless puzzling, she would probably have threatened to appeal to the policeman. So I took the other line.

I overtook her and tapped her on the shoulder. "This kind of thing cannot be allowed," I said sharply.

She was obviously much flustered and confused.

"Oh, what do you mean, sir?" she said.

"You know very well what I mean. I have had you under observation for some time—in the train and in the lift."

"Yes—oh, yes. I remember. I didn't know I was doing anything actually wrong."

"Absolutely illegal. I'm afraid I must do my duty."

"Oh, please don't!" she said. "I can explain everything if you'll listen. If you took me to a police-station, you'd only find you'd made a mistake. And the publicity of it would kill me; I've been fighting against publicity all my life."

I saw, of course, that she had mistaken me for a detective acting in the interests of the Post Office. I had thought she might make that mistake. It would have broken my tailor's heart, but for the moment I did not correct it.

"Very well," I said. "We'll step aside into the park. But I must have the whole truth, and the explanation must be satisfactory to me."

"I'm sure you will find it so. And I'm very much obliged to you. I will tell you the whole thing from beginning to end."

As we crossed the grass to the chairs under the trees, she said: "I've only done it twice before, and I didn't know there was any real harm in it, but I'll never, never do it again."

As I was not quite sure what she was talking about, I said that I hoped she wouldn't. We sat down, and I lit a cigarette. She was clearly relieved that I was dealing so leniently with her.

"Now, then, madam," I said. "From the beginning, please."

"I am a widow," she said. "I do not know whether the name will suggest anything to you, but I am Mrs. Sumple."

I had seen the name frequently in shops and in advertisements. "Yes," I said, "it does suggest something to me; it suggests a disinfectant."

"I expected it," she said, with a sigh. "Sumple's Liquid Safety is but too well known. My poor husband invented it."

"Surely," I said, "the more it is known, the better, from a commercial point of view, it must be for you, then."

"That—unfortunately, is not so. When I married Arbuthnot Sumple, he held an honourable salaried post as analyst to an important manufacturing firm—Shadwell and Joy, the soapmakers. The disinfectant was invented by him in his leisure time, and it was he, I regret to say, who thought of the name for it. But he had no means other than his salary, and was in consequence unable to place the thing on the market. Somebody had to be found who, for a small share in the profits, would provide the money for manufacturing the disinfectant and for advertising it and pushing it with the trade. So naturally I thought of Mr. Magwhit."

"Magwhit," I observed, "is a name known and respected in the lesser financial world. But why was it specially natural that you should select him?"

"Simply and solely because he married my cousin Clara. She was a Miss Bone before marriage, and, of course, everybody says that she has a very charming manner. That may be, but she is not always sincere and she can also be very unpleasant. Well, I said to poor dear Arbuthnot: 'There is only one thing to be done—we must get at Percy Magwhit through Clara.' I am sorry to say that my husband took my advice. Arbuthnot was not a business man; Magwhit was. You can imagine the result."

"I can, Mrs. Sumple. The financier swallowed the inventor. That generally happens."

"Precisely. Sumple's Liquid Safety did not do very well the first six months, and not much better the next six. Arbuthnot was weak and got discouraged. Mr. Magwhit made him an offer, and he accepted it. He sold all his rights in Sumple's Liquid Safety for an annuity—four hundred a year for his life and mine. And at the time I really thought Mr. Magwhit was treating him generously. That was only four years ago. Yet last year Mr. Magwhit made no less than thirty thousand pounds out of the disinfectant, and this year, as Clara admits, he will make still more."

"It seems hard," I said.

"It is very hard, sir. My income from my husband's salary vanished, of course, at his death, and he was not insured. I have only the four hundred a year, and I have all the odium from the disinfectant. The Magwhits have thirty thousand a year from it, and no odium at all. I shall never get used to the horrible publicity of the thing. My name stares at me from a hoarding, and it is a shock. A newspaper advertisement tells me to be sure it is Sumple's, and I shudder. I go into a chemist's shop, and some young man enters and demands Sumple in the eighteenpenny size, and I blush to the roots of my hair. My name serves as a mudguard to protect the Magwhits. I doubt if any of the smart people that Clara entertains in Hill Street or at Tufmore know that the Magwhits have ever dabbled in disinfectants at all."

"Well," I said, "if you don't like it, it is a very simple matter to change your name."

"Never!" she said, and the jet trimming on her frontage trembled with emotion. "That is a piece of treachery to Arbuthnot's memory that I can never commit. I would sooner suffer as I do. The Magwhits might change the name of the disinfectant, but when I suggest it, they smile and change the subject."

"That is quite likely. But, Mrs. Sumple, you promised me an explanation of certain curious facts that I have observed. What bearing has all this on—"

"Everything can be traced to it, as you will see, and you asked me to begin at the beginning. I have this reduced income of four hundred a year. Fortunately, I have no children and nobody dependent on me. Even as it is, I have the greatest difficulty in keeping up the very modest style to which I am accustomed, without getting into debt. My little flat in Upper Gloucester Place is expensive. I think it a fairly good address myself, though Clara lets me see that she considers it contemptible, and pretended, when I took it, that she did not know where it was."

"One moment. You have not quarrelled with Mrs. Magwhit, then? You are still on good terms with her?"

"We are quite intimate, yet we dislike one another. That may surprise you."

"On the contrary, it is one of the commonest combinations."

"We played together as children, and have known each other all our lives. So, though I considered her husband cheated mine, I have not dropped her. To be candid, I have always had hopes that he might, in consequence of the great prosperity of the disinfectant, suggest something in the way of a bonus. I have already given hints in that direction. As Clara always, until her marriage, had to help in the housework in the morning, it was perfectly absurd of her to pretend that she had never heard of Upper Gloucester Place. But she can be kind when she likes. She has occasionally asked me to receptions in Hill Street, and although I never know anybody there, and cannot afford the dress expenditure and the cab fares, I should be sorry to miss them. She has frequently invited me to luncheon when only she and the governess have been present. And she did once ask me down to Tufmore. I had to be postponed, as my room was wanted for Lady Rochester's maid; but that I quite understood, and no doubt at some other time—"

"Pardon me, Mrs. Sumple, but is this really explanatory?"

"In a way it is. It shows that I have expensive friends, and that explains why I have had to look about me for methods of making money. I had thought about home-made pickles, but people in the other flats would have objected to the smell of vinegar. And Clara refused to push them with her friends, and said that nobody but the servants ever eat pickles. I am earning a commission for recommending Gimlong Tea, or, at any rate, I shall be as soon as I get some orders. I wrote a testimonial for the Bestwear Boot and Shoe Company in Orchard Street the other day, but there was no agreement, and all I received was one complimentary pair of walking shoes. And then I turned my attention to silkworms."

"Silkworms?"

"Yes, I'll tell you how it happened. My charwoman brought them to me in a little box. She said her son had got them from another boy, and he would sell them for sixpence. She had been told that the silk they made fetched fabulous prices. Naturally, I bought them. There were a hundred and eight of them originally, and it seemed a good bargain. Where I was wrong was in not inquiring about their food."

"You had trouble about it?"

"I did. I tried them with lettuce, which rabbits and almost all animals like. Nineteen of them died that night. Despair drove me to experiment with bread-crumbs, and fifty-three more of the poor creatures perished in the next twenty-four hours. This morning the charwoman came again, and said that I ought to feed them on mulberry leaves. Now, I have no mulberry tree in my flat, and so I thought the best thing I could do was to cut my loss and give the silkworms to one of the lift-men at Baker Street Station. He was a man who had been most civil and obliging, and I had always wanted to make him some little present. I went from Baker Street Station. I was wearing, only for the second time, the complimentary shoes that the Bestwear Company had sent me. There was the lift just on the point of starting, and the particular lift-man I wanted was in it. I made a rush for it, and I suppose I caught the heel of one of my shoes in something. At any rate, the heel came clean off and went spinning across the floor of the booking-office. I did not wait to pick it up, or I should have missed the lift. But I told the lift-man about it, and asked him, if anybody found the heel, to have it reserved for me. I then offered him the silkworms, but he said he did not understand their habits and couldn't take them. I was explaining to him my difficulty, when suddenly something which Clara once said to me flashed across my mind. 'Wait,' I said; 'I know a lady who has a mulberry tree. I will take the silk-worms to her.' Do you see?"

"I am beginning to see."

"The hats in the shops were most extraordinary. There was one at Pigwell's which it is no exaggeration to say—"

"Pardon," I said, "you can leave out the part about the hats. If I surmise correctly, you went on to Mrs. Magwhit's, in Hill Street."

"I did. I had to. Silkworms apart, it was quite imperative. The strain on my ankles! You perhaps do not know what it is to walk with a high heel on one shoe and none at all on the other. It gives one a curious gait, which is remarked and quite misunderstood by boys in the street, and it is painful as well. Uncertain though I was of the way Clara would take it, I felt I must borrow a pair of shoes from her. Otherwise, I should have been driven to take a cab, and that is an expense which I always try to avoid. I found Clara at home—you can imagine her, perhaps."

"Not in the least."

"No? Then I must tell you. She has a beautiful and graceful figure—I will say that for her—and she dresses like an Egyptian serpent and is rather languid. As a matter of fact, she is quite keen in matters of business. She writes all the advertisements of Sumple's Liquid Safety, and had proofs of some new handbills on the table in her boudoir when I went in. Her manner this morning was what might be called medium. I have known her to be more affectionate, and I have known her to be nastier. She said that of course I could have a pair of her shoes if I could get into them—her foot is a half-size larger than mine, and she is sensitive about it—but she couldn't think why I bought rotten shoes that dropped to pieces in the street. She showed me the new handbills. There was a blank space where there was to be a picture, and underneath was printed 'Sumple's Liquid Safety is Death to all Disease Germs.' So I said I had something to show her, too—something that she might like to buy from me—and I handed her the box of silkworms. She opened it, screamed, and lost her temper. She said it was disgusting of me to bring a box of dead maggots and mess into her house. What was I thinking of? Had I gone mad? Well, I did my best to appease her.

I told her I was sorry, but they were not maggots; they were silk-worms—pretty, playful little things—and some of them were still alive. However, I would take them away as soon as I got my shoes on. She seemed pacified, and said I could have one of the hand-bills to wrap the box in."

"I see," I said. "You wrapped the box in the handbill. That accounts for the legend on the box. But what about your shoes? They are of different colours."

"Really, you notice everything!"

"Everything which is unusual and nothing which is not."

"Well I will tell you. All Clara's shoes are bronze green and so are all her stockings, and they have to match exactly; it is one of her fads and affectations. As I was putting on the right-hand shoe, I told Clara that the real reason why I had brought the silkworms to her was because I remembered her saying that there was a mulberry tree on the front lawn at Tufmore, and this would have made it quite easy for her to feed them. Clara sighed and said I had got the most unaccountable delusions. The tree was a sycamore, and she had never told me that it was anything else, if she had ever mentioned it at all, which she did not believe. Of course, that may have been so. All I can say is that, if it was not Clara who said she had a mulberry tree, then it must have been somebody else. However, to change the subject, I asked her what she was going to have for the picture on the new handbill. 'Oh,' she said, 'I don't know. Some funny old face, I think. We might have the widow of the inventor!" Well, that was enough for me. There are things which I permit and things which I do not permit. Clara had passed the limit. I simply got up and walked out. She told me not to be a fool and take offence at a joke, but, as I said to her, there are jokes and jokes. When I got into the street, I remembered that I had changed only one of my shoes, but I would not go back. And now, sir, I have told you everything fully and frankly."

"Pardon me, Mrs. Sumple. I understand now why you are wearing odd shoes. Your curious conversation with the lift-man is also explained—by the way, I am sorry that you did not get the heel of your shoe back—but why did you post the silkworms?" "Well, sir, I had to get rid of them, and what else was I to do? There was nowhere else to put them. If I had dropped them in the street, somebody would have picked them up and brought them back to me, and very likely a reward would have been expected. Seeing all I have gone through, I am sure, sir, you must admit that I have been sufficiently punished."

"But I think you said that on two previous occasions you have used a pillar-box in the same reprehensible way—in fact, as a dustbin?"

"Yes, but it will never happen again. In one case I had bought something from the fishmonger and was taking it home myself. I had practically told him that it must be fresh, and I never dealt with him again. In the other case it was—well, it was a mistake of my dentist's. I wished to get rid of it, and I was anxious from delicate motives that it should not be traced to me. I could not burn it, but I could and did post it. Of course, I did not know that the Post Office employed detectives to watch the pillar-boxes."

"Nor did I."

"But you are a detective yourself? You said so."

"There, Mrs. Sumple, you are mistaken. I said that I had had you under observation for some time, and it was true. I pointed out that you could not be allowed to throw refuse into pillar-boxes, nor can you. I did say that I must do my duty, and England expects every man to do as much, but I never said I was a detective, and I never should say it. Why, it's illegal!"

"Then, if you are not a detective, what are you?"

"Merely," I said, "an old gentleman who employs an ample leisure in the satisfaction of an inquiring and curious disposition. Thank you very much indeed, Mrs. Sumple, and good morning." I left her still searching for words to express her feelings. But she quickly recovered herself and came panting after me.

"Gimlong Tea," she said breathlessly. "Splendid tea. Under the circumstances, I think you must give me an order."

In the Marmalade

I took the eleven o'clock Pullman for Brighton one Sunday morning, and entered the train twenty minutes before it started.

On the opposite side of the car to myself two men were seated. One of them was an elderly gentleman, with a neatly trimmed white beard, and from his face I judged him to be both wise and kind. I gathered that he was not going on in the train, and had merely entered it for a few minutes' chat with his companion. This latter was a much younger man, not more than twenty-five. He was a good-looking boy, and he seemed worried and even slightly excited. It was evident that he employed a first-rate tailor and bootmaker, and I think he gave fifteen shillings for his ordinary straw hat. His taste in clothes was quiet and correct, and I was a little surprised that he spoiled the set of a well-cut coat—he was wearing a dark blue lounge suit—by carrying a heavy pocket-book or something of that kind in the inner side-pocket.

"I've made up my mind," he said, a little irritably, "and it's no good to worry any more about it. I'm going to put it in her marmalade."

"Don't do it," said the older man anxiously. "I beg you not to do it. The consequences—"

"There won't be any consequences—at least, there won't be any of the kind you mean. I tell you Parton did the same thing, and he swears there's no risk whatever. Discovery is practically impossible."

"I don't like it," said the old gentleman. "And I wish you had never told me about it, for it haunts me. You haven't even got the excuse of poverty."

"Perhaps not; but I'm not going to chuck money away, all the same."

"It might, I believe, lead to your arrest and—"

"Hush!" said the young man in a low voice. He had, I think, noticed that the conversation was being overheard by me.

They talked for a minute or two, and then the old gentleman shook hands and left the train. The only other phrase which I could catch was "probably in the *Lusitania*."

I have frequently been called a curious and interfering old man. It is certainly true that I take an interest in anything which interests me, and that I have the strongest dislike to being left with only part of a story. I meant, if I could, to get at the rest of the story in this case. I changed my seat, after complaining of a draught to the attendant, and took the seat opposite the young man. There was a small table in between us, and we were now within conversational range. But I did not hurry matters; for a time I read my paper sedulously, and appeared to take no notice of my young friend.

Presently he told the attendant to bring him a whisky and soda, and, in paying for his drink, he dropped a florin, which finally came to rest under my seat. I rescued it and handed it back to him. He thanked me politely, and said he was sorry to have given me the trouble.

"Oh, it was no trouble," I said. "Beautiful morning, isn't it?"

"Yes, pretty good."

"I wonder if it's impertinent for a stranger to say it—but I'm an old man, and old men notice such things—but I couldn't help being struck just now with the likeness between your father and yourself."

"Really? My father died about sixteen years ago."

"Ah, then it was not your father! My mistake. Stupid of me! I suppose one doesn't observe correctly when one is mentally preoccupied. And all the time I was puzzling over another point connected with you."

"Well?" said the young man grudgingly.

"Speaking frankly," I said, "and with my assurance on my word of honour that it shall go no further, what is it that you intend to put in her marmalade?"

His face showed how angry he was. "I think, sir," he said, "that you would do better to mind your own business!" He snatched up a newspaper from the table and opened it out between us.

"Funny you should tell me to mind my own business," I said placidly. "So many people have told me that. And as a matter of fact, I have no business—no profession or occupation of any kind." He made no answer whatever. Rather rude, I thought, seeing how very much younger he was than myself. I waited a few minutes, and then said—

"I don't want to hurry you, but you'll let me have my newspaper back when you've quite finished with it, won't you?" I had noticed that inadvertently he had picked up my newspaper. He flung the newspaper down on the table, said a wicked word, finished his whisky and soda hurriedly, and went out. I think he found a seat in the next car; he did not return. I caught a glimpse of him at Brighton station as he drove away in a cab. And then I strolled up to the Metropole to lunch with friends of mine who were stopping there.

For the moment I did not see anything further to be done. I put the problem by for further consideration, with not much hope that I should ever be able to work it out.

Shortly after three that afternoon, it seemed to me wicked to keep my friends awake any longer—they had, I knew, the after-luncheon-snooze habit—and I left the hotel, and started on to the West Pier. And there, seated in a deck-chair, with his back towards me, I found the young man who had been so unpardonably rude to me that morning. As I was looking at his back, he got up and strolled off. Something may be learned by the student of human backs. This young man had a dejected back. I followed him, but without any intention of overtaking him and tackling him again.

As I passed the chair where he had sat, I noticed on the seat of it a green leather case which might very well have caused that bulge in his pocket which I had noticed in the train. I sat down in that chair and opened the case.

The case contained a large diamond star. They were good white diamonds, and the thing would have cost a hundred pounds or very little less. Having satisfied myself as to its contents, I put it in my pocket, and, leaning back in the chair, closed my eyes in thought.

How could I piece the clues together? I went over them in my mind—diamonds, marmalade, a making or saving of money, a possibility of arrest, the *Lusitania*. And suddenly the whole explanation seemed to flash out at me. I take no credit for any peculiar cleverness about it, for I had heard of a similar fraud on the American Customs before. All I had to do now was to wait in the neighbourhood of that deck-chair for my man to come back. I imagined—correctly, as the event showed—that he had taken the case from his pocket to look at the diamonds, and in replacing it had missed the pocket, and allowed the case to slip down between his coat and waistcoat. He would probably feel for those diamonds again in a few minutes, would find they were missing, and would return to see if he had dropped the case where he was sitting. I now stood a few yards away from the deck-chair, with my back to it, looking out over the sea. I heard that the deck-chair was being moved, and steps going to and fro and round and round just behind me, but I did not turn my head until I heard the young man speaking to me. He was very polite this time.

"I beg your pardon, sir. I'm extremely sorry to trouble you, but while I was sitting here a few minutes ago I most carelessly allowed a green leather case to slip out of my pocket. The contents were valuable. I suppose you don't happen to have seen it?"

"You were extremely rude to me in the train this morning, sir. I am not disposed to help you in any way."

"Sorry if I seemed rude. I was a bit out of temper at the time. That old bore who came to see me off had been bothering me with a lot of good advice on my private affairs, and I didn't want to discuss them any further. If you have seen my case—"

"But how am I to know that it was your case? The person who took— But I'd better say nothing about it."

The young man had hurriedly pulled a paper from his pocket. "If you'll just look at that—it is the receipt from the shop where I bought the thing—it proves my ownership."

I glanced over the paper perfunctorily. "This tells me that, if you are the Reginald Wing, Esquire, here mentioned, you bought a diamond star. Nothing is said about the green leather case. And the person who took it did so very deliberately—no sign of nervousness, not the appearance of a thief at all."

"I am Mr. Wing," he said, and he was beautifully patient, "and the case is never mentioned in the bill. It contained the diamond star described there. I've already apologized for my abruptness this morning, and in a business like this every moment is of importance. If you'll give me a description of the man who picked up that case—"

"Pardon me, I never said it was a man. I said a person."

"What? Was it a woman? Young? Red hair? Rather—"

"You are asking me a great many questions. This morning you refused to answer one of mine."

"Well, tell me all you know about my diamonds, and I'll tell you everything about the marmalade." That was the sentence I had been waiting for. "You are very good," I said, "but I already know about the marmalade."

"That," he said, "is absolutely impossible."

"It may appear so to you."

"If you'll first tell me who took my diamonds, and give me the time to see the police about recovering them, I'll hear your explanation and bet you a sovereign it is wrong. And if it is wrong, I will put you right. Will that suit you?"

"Perfectly. We might sit down, I think. It was I who took your diamonds."

"Great Scot, why didn't you say so?"

"Why didn't you ask me? Delicacy, perhaps. However, here they are, quite safe, as you will see, please."

He was full of gratitude, and mighty glad to get that diamond star back again.

"And now, Mr. Wing," I said, "I'll proceed to win that sovereign from you. My name's Fish—Horace Fish—and as I have nothing else to do, I devote a good deal of time to solving the Chinese puzzles that the lives and private affairs of other people present to me. And with much practice I have gained a certain facility. That is why I have succeeded in doing what you thought impossible."

"I still think it impossible, Mr. Fish."

"We shall see. The clues in my possession, mostly derived from scraps of conversation overheard, were these—marmalade, in which something was to be put, diamonds, the *Lusitania*, an attempt to save money, and a possibility of serious consequences, perhaps arrest. Does not the order in which I have put these things already suggest to you that I have hit the right nail on the head?"

"No," said Mr. Wing.

"Well, you shall hear the whole story. You wish to send a diamond star to a lady at present resident in America. You wish to avoid the very high tariff on articles of this kind, and therefore you are going to use a dodge which a friend of yours, Parton by name, has already employed with success. You intend to conceal the star in a tin or jar of marmalade. You may send this in the ordinary way, but it seems to me more probable that you mean to entrust it to a friend who is crossing on the *Lusitania*. It is quite true that you will save money if your fraud is not detected. But I think the old gentleman who was with you in the train was quite right in warning you. Customs officers occasionally employ an investigatory skewer. If they used it on that marmalade, you would lose a great deal more money than the sum you propose to save."

"That," said Reginald Wing, "is about the most ingenious thing I ever heard. I could never have worked it out like that. I congratulate you, sir."

"And, if I remember correctly, you pay me a sovereign."

"Oh no, Mr. Fish—not at all! You pay me the sovereign. Your story is most ingenious, and if ever I want to send precious stones to America, I may be able to make some practical use of it, But it's not right—in fact, it's all wrong from beginning to end. Now, the right story—"

"Yes," I said, feeling for my sovereign case, "what is it?"

"Quite simple. Miss Judd, who was housekeeper to my Uncle Ambrose during his lifetime, is, and always has been, one of the kindest and best-natured of women. As a boy of fourteen I owed much to her. Ever since, I have liked her and she has liked me. She is about fifteen years older than myself, and I have always regarded her as a kind of supernumerary aunt. Mark you, even in my boyhood's days she frequently bought sweets with the intention of presenting them to me, but was unable to resist the temptation to eat them herself."

"I don't quite see what this has to do with it."

"It has everything to do with it. When my Uncle Ambrose died— a little more than a year ago—no mention was made of me in his will. We had never quarrelled. He had told me definitely that I should get between seven and eight thousand when he was gone, and that my three cousins would get the same. Only a few days before his death he told Miss Judd that this was what he had done, and spoke of me with affection. The will was not very well drawn, and I am convinced that the omission of my name was either a queer error of memory or a clerical oversight. That also was Miss Judd's view. He provided for my three cousins just as he had told me. To Miss Judd herself he left six hundred pounds a year for life, the money to go to his favourite hospital after her death. You have grasped these points, Mr. Fish? They are important."

"Yes, I understand."

"Very well. As soon as she knew the terms of the will, Miss Judd came to me in the greatest distress. Either I was to take half her income of six hundred pounds, or she would renounce the whole thing. She had no one dependent on her, and her tastes and habits would not require even three hundred pounds a year. She was convinced that my omission had been inadvertent, and that she would be carrying out the real wishes of my uncle. Under the pressure she brought to bear, I consented to receive three hundred pounds a year from her. Now, this income will cease when her life ceases. Also, as she puts by money every year, and will leave the whole of it to me, the longer she lives the more I shall receive. Quite apart from ordinary humanity and the great affection I have for her, I have the most solid reasons for wishing Miss Judd to live as long as possible. But a most deplorable thing has happened. Good-natured people are generally lazy, and Miss Judd is no exception.

Since my uncle's death she has refused to take up with any definite occupation. Her fatal passion for sweets has increased, and she has been mad enough to take a suite of rooms immediately over a high-class confectioner's shop. She never cared about exercise, and never walked a step farther than she could help. The change has come with alarming rapidity. I saw her last week for the first time for six months, and she has become enormous. She breathes with difficulty; her heart is giving her trouble. She has consulted a doctor, who allows her to take no specific for obesity, but has put her on a strict diet. I believe she does make some attempt to adhere to that diet, but the attempt is, and will continue to be, a hopeless failure. With the confectioner's shop at hand, what else could you expect? She has faith in her doctor, and, except in the matter of diet, would not dream of disobeying his orders. Am I to let that woman die? Polden's Emaciatory Powders are colourless, harmless, almost tasteless. If I conceal them in the marmalade which she eats to excess every morning for breakfast, she will recover in spite of herself. You see?"

"I do. You risk a great deal."

"No risk at all. Parton and his two sisters have used them without ill effects of any kind—on the contrary, with great benefit to their health."

"That proves nothing. You have, it seems to me, an insurable interest in this lady's life. Why did you not insure it?"

"Do young men ever think of insurance? I did not until it was too late. No insurance company would accept Miss Judd now on any terms."

"And the diamonds—the mention of the *Lusitania*?"

"Had nothing whatever to do with it. I had intended to present these diamonds to-day to a young lady. For reasons which do not concern you, I have not given them to her."

"But, my dear Mr. Wing, everything concerns me."

"Very well, then. If you were lunching with a girl at a restaurant, and you found a dish so bad that you called up the manager and had it changed, and the girl in the manager's presence called you a silly idiot, and asked for a second helping of the same dish, would you think that she showed the kind of temper that promised happiness in the married life?"

"I should not."

"Nor did I. The reference to the *Lusitania* was quite accidental— a brother of mine is going out there on business. I think that's all."

I handed him the sovereign. "And," I said, "would you, as a favour, let me have two lines to say the result of your experiment with Miss Judd."

"Certainly. But I have not your address."

I gave him my card, and we parted. I thought that this would be a lesson to me in future not to decide too hurriedly that any particular thing amounted to a clue.

Next day I received the following letter:

"Dear Sir,—In return for the service you rendered me, I promised to tell you the true explanation of the conversation which you overheard. I did not say when I would do it, but I choose to do it now. Observing in the train that you were making the utmost effort to overhear what my uncle and myself were saying, I thought I would give you something for your trouble. An almost imperceptible wink to my uncle accompanied my remark that I would put it in her marmalade, and my dear old uncle is fairly quick at the up-take. You followed up beautifully.

"Briefly, you have been spoofed. Miss Judd and Uncle Ambrose and the Emaciatory Powder are but parts of a myth. My story about the diamonds and the girl was also spoof. So sorry, but you deserved it.

"Faithfully yours,
"Reginald Wing."

People seem to think that if you deserve a thing, you must like to get it. This is not invariably the case. I tell the story because it shows that even the cleverest may occasionally fail.

THE PROBLEM CLUB

No. I
The Giraffe Problem

The general public knows little about the Problem Club. Many are not even aware that it has now been in existence for several years. Nor can it be said that the references to it which have appeared from time to time in the Press have been very enlightening, or even reasonably accurate.

For instance, a paragraph in a recent issue of a society paper (which, it may be admitted, is generally well informed) makes various statements as to the Problem Club. It says that the club has its premises underground in Piccadilly, that a former Premier is a member of it, that all the members are required to swear a most solemn oath to act with scrupulous honour in the monthly competitions, and that high play frequently goes on. The actual truth is that there are no club premises. The famous but old-fashioned restaurant that reserves two rooms on the first floor for the club's monthly meetings is not situated in Piccadilly. No Premier has ever been a member. The story of the solemn oath is even more absurd. After all, the members are gentlemen. They would as soon think of taking a solemn oath not to cheat at cards or at golf. The "scrupulous honour" is taken for granted. Lastly, there is no high play in the accepted sense of the term. The amount that a member can win or lose in the monthly competitions will be stated presently, and any betting on the results is prohibited.

Silly misrepresentations of this kind have caused some annoyance, and it is now thought that a discreet but authorised

45

account of some part of the proceedings of the club would be preferable.

The club consists of twelve members, and the annual subscription is one hundred and thirty-four pounds. Of this sum twenty-four pounds is allotted to the club expenses, including the club dinners which are held on the first Saturday in every month. Each member in turn acts as chairman at one dinner in the year, afterwards adjudicating upon the problem competition for that month; while at the other eleven meetings he is himself a competitor, the remaining one hundred and ten pounds of his subscription being treated as eleven entrance fees of ten pounds each. The problems are not of a mathematical nature, and were for some time invented and propounded by Leonard, the ingenious head-waiter of the restaurant. The winner receives the whole of the entrance fees, amounting to one hundred and ten pounds; if there is more than one winner this amount is divided equally between them. Thus for his investment of one hundred and ten pounds it is possible that a member may in one year obtain a return of one thousand two hundred and ten pounds, if he is the sole winner of the eleven competitions for which he is eligible. But the minute-books of the club show that in actual practice this has never happened; indeed, the record, made by Mr. Pusely-Smythe in 1911, is seven wins, and on two occasions out of the seven he had to share the prize with another successful competitor.

It may be admitted that the club has necessarily been of the nature of a secret society. Some of the problems set have been rather curious, and it has occasionally happened that in the course of their practical solution members have been led to do things which might prejudice them in their domestic or social relations, or even subject them to the penalties of the law.

It is permitted to add an account of some of the pre-war meetings of the club, various natural precautions being taken to prevent the discovery of the identity of members.

It was the forty-third meeting of the Problem Club. Dinner was over, and the members had adjourned to the lofty and comfortable room where the business of the evening was transacted. A side-table was suitably equipped with provision for smokers—all the members were smokers—and for such other refreshments as might be required in the course of the evening. One or two waiters still lingered— removing a coffee-cup, handing a liqueur, or placing an ash-tray and matches conveniently on one of the small tables. A hum of conversation went on through the blue haze of the cigar-smoke. Mr. Pusely-Smythe, with his usual lugubrious manner, was just coming to the end of a screamingly funny story. Any reference to the competition to be settled is by an unwritten law forbidden until the chairman has opened the proceedings, but it was noticeable that Major Byles was once more talking of resigning his membership. He was not taken very seriously. He was an original member, and, though he lived in the country for the greater part of the year, had never been known to miss a single meeting of the club. His continuous bad luck in the competitions had irritated him, but nobody believed in his threat of resignation, and it may be doubted if he quite believed in it himself.

The waiters left the room, and Sir Charles Bunford, an elderly gentleman of distinguished appearance, who was chairman for the evening, took his place at his table and arranged his papers. Among them the club cheque-book showed temptingly. In accordance with the club custom by which the chairman at one meeting acted as secretary at the next, Dr. Alden took his seat beside Sir Charles and prepared to make a note of the proceedings for the club minute-book. Conversation ceased. The other members seated themselves informally in a semicircle of easy-chairs. There was, indeed, a marked absence of formality at the Problem Club. There was no order of precedence. The chairman did not rise when he spoke, nor did members rise when they answered him.

"Now, gentlemen," Sir Charles began, "we have before us to-night the Giraffe Problem. I will read it out to you as worded by our esteemed friend Leonard: 'It is required to induce a woman who is unaware of your intention to say to you, "You ought to have been a giraffe."' Now, of course, I'm not a competitor, but I must say that I'm sorry I'm not. Upon my word, I don't think Leonard has ever given us anything quite so easy."

There were several dissentient voices: "Not a bit of it." "Can't agree with you there, Bunford." "Wish I'd found it so." "Leonard knew what he was doing this time."

"Oh, very well," said Sir Charles smiling. "I should have thought there were a score of conversational openings to which the inevitable reply would be, 'You ought to have been a giraffe.' I may be wrong, but I still expect that the prize to-night will have to be divided between four or five of you. However, we'll see what luck you've had. I'll begin with you, doctor, and then go on in the direction of the sun and the wine."

Dr. Alden shook his head. He had a strong head, an alert expression, and a bright eye. "No good," he said. "There was too much to do in Harley Street this month for me to be able to give the proper time to it. I made an attempt. It has probably cost me the esteem of an excellent woman; these excellent women never think you're serious except when you're joking. I gave her the chance to tell me I ought to have been a giraffe, but she never took it. Enough said. Try the next man."

"The next is our only member of Parliament, Mr. Harding Pope."

"Not competing this month," said Mr. Pope rather pompously. "My constituency has made great demands upon me, and I'm unable to defend my entrance fee. Fortunately, the pleasure of the company in which I find myself is worth far more."

"That's all right," said Sir Charles warningly, "but don't get too slack. We've got a long waiting list. What about you, Major Byles?"

"My usual luck," said the Major. "I worked the whole thing out completely and made all the necessary preparations. I was down at my cottage at the time. I assure you that during the whole of breakfast one morning I talked about practically nothing except giraffes and the way that they can pull down fruit from a tree, thanks to their thundering long necks. My wife, the children's governess, and Mrs. Hebor, who was stopping with us, all heard me, though I can't say that they seemed particularly interested. Afterwards my wife and I were in the garden, and I pointed to a tree full of ripe cherries.

"'I like fruit,' I said, 'but I hate climbing trees.'

"Now, considering the ground-bait that I had been putting down at breakfast, I consider the betting was ten to one that she would reply that I ought to have been a giraffe. Instead of that, she said that Wilkins would get them for me, and then seemed surprised that I was annoyed. A few minutes later I tried the governess with precisely the same remark, and she asked me if I would like to have a ladder fetched. (I often wonder what I pay that woman her salary for.) Then Mrs. Hebor came out—as dependable a woman as I know in a general way; you nearly always know what she is going to say before she says it—and I told her that I liked cherries, but hated climbing to get them.

"'You ought,' she began—and this time I thought I really had got it—'to be able to reach some of those without climbing.'

"After that I gave up. No amount of intelligence can contend against luck like that. Matter of fact, I'm tempted to give up this problem business altogether."

"Oh, don't do that," said Sir Charles soothingly. "It was hard lines, but we shall see you a prize-winner one of these days. Now, Mr. Cunliffe, what have you to tell us?"

"I failed," said the Rev. Septimus Cunliffe, an elderly cleric who specialised in broadmindedness. "Plausible strategy, but disappointing results. Nothing of interest to report."

"Did you do any better, Mr. Matthews?"

Mr. Matthews was a man of forty, bald, round-faced, rubicund, and slightly obese. The task of ordering the club dinners and the wines to be drunk therewith was always left in his hands with a confidence which was invariably justified. His knowledge as an epicure was considerable, and it is possible that his intelligence was less considerable, but more than once he had been lucky in a competition. He was the richest man in a club where nobody was very poor, and was good-tempered and popular.

"Well, you know," said Matthews, "I feel as if I ought to have won this. At one time it looked as if I simply had it chucked at me. I was talking to Lady Amelia, who does a lot in the East End and is always nosing round for subscriptions.

"'Why do you men drink?' she asked in her blunt way.

"The question of this competition occurred to me, and it looked like a good chance.

"'Well,' I said, 'the pleasure begins in the palate, but I fancy that it continues in the throat. I often wish I had a longer throat.'

"You would have hardly thought she could have missed it, but she did. Said that she was sure I was not so bad as I made myself out to be, and milked me of a fiver for some rotten 'good cause.'"

"Look here," said Major Byles, returning from a fruitless visit to the side-table, "I'll ask the chairman for a minute's interval. They've not put out any seltzer, though they must know that I always take seltzer with mine."

"Certainly, Major; certainly. Would somebody kindly touch the bell?"

The seltzer-water was brought and business was resumed.

"Your turn next, Jimmy," said Sir Charles.

The Hon. James Feldane, a rather weary young man, said, "Well, I claim to be a winner, but there's a shade of doubt about it, and I'll ask for your ruling. All I can say is that if I don't touch the money my luck's even worse than the Major's. Like him, I was systematic about it. My first step was to buy some of the highest collars that could be got for money—two inches or so too high for me and beastly uncomfortable. I put one of them on, and looked like a bad freak— something out of a back number of *Punch*. My next step was to call on my married sister. She told me to go home and dress myself properly, as I knew she would. So I asked in my innocent way what was wrong, and she said I seemed to have mistaken my neck for the Nelson Column.

"'Alluding to my collar?' I said. 'Well, I like plenty. I'd wear a collar three feet high if I could.'"

"And then my fool of a brother-in-law stuck his oar in, and said, 'You ought to have been a giraffe'; and I'm absolutely certain Dora would have said it if he hadn't got in first.

"So there it is—the words were all right, but they were used by a man. Still, for some purposes—bankruptcy and things of that kind—a man and his wife count as one, don't they? What's the ruling?"

"My ruling," said Sir Charles, "is that your claim fails. It is required that the words should be used by a woman, and your brother-in-law is not a woman."

"Yes, I was afraid you'd think so," said Jimmy, "but it was worth trying. Anybody want any rotten high collars?"

"Now, Mr. Pusely-Smythe," said the chairman.

Mr. Pusely-Smythe was a man of middle age, with dark, cavernous eyes and an intellectual forehead. He was pale and thin, and was less solemn than he seemed.

"I claim to have won," he said in a melancholy voice. "My method was not the most obvious or direct, and might easily have failed, but the luck was with me. I must tell you that I happen to know a Mrs. Magsworth, who of late years has given way a good deal to Nature Study. She haunts the Zoo and the Botanical Gardens. She understands about the habitat of the hyena, and if cockroaches devour their young, and which end of the tree the onion grows—all that kind of thing. She is rather severe with people who, as she phrases it, 'show an abysmal ignorance of the simplest facts.' She has got a face like a horse, though that is not germane to the question. I arranged with a kindly hostess to let me take in Mrs. Magsworth to dinner one evening—I gather that there was no particular rush for the job.

"I said: 'I'm so glad to meet you again, Mrs. Magsworth. With your knowledge you will be able to settle a point that has been worrying me for days. My little nephew asked me which was the tallest animal. And, do you know, I couldn't be quite sure.'

"'Then, Mr. Smythe,' she said, 'you ought to have been. A giraffe is much the tallest of the mammals.'

"So I claim to have won. She, being a woman ignorant of my intention, was induced to say to me the words required in the order required and without the interpolation of any other word."

"But there's the interpolation of a full stop," said Mr. Harding Pope, and was at once called to order—only the chairman has the right to comment and to adjudicate.

Sir Charles took a few moments to consider his decision, and then gave his ruling as follows:—

"My ruling is that Mr. Pusely-Smythe's claim is conditionally allowed. It is true that Mrs. Magsworth used other words both before and after the words required, but that is not precluded by the terms of the problem. The only other possible objection is that there was the interpolation of a full stop. Now, there is no full stop in spoken speech: it is represented by a pause. In this case the pause indicated the end of a sentence. In another case the pause might have indicated that the woman could not for a moment think of the word giraffe. In that case I am sure that no objection would have been raised. Yet there, too, a sign could be used to represent it in print or writing. Leonard requires certain words in a certain order, but he does not forbid a pause to be made between them. Unless some member has induced a woman to use the same words with no pause whatever—which I should rule to be a still better solution—Mr. Pusely-Smythe's claim is allowed."

As no other member had met with any success at all, a cheque for one hundred and ten pounds was drawn to the order of Mr. Pusely-Smythe and handed to him with the congratulations of the chairman.

The chairman's next duty was to open the sealed envelope containing the problem set by the ingenious Leonard for the ensuing month. This was entitled "The Kiss Problem," and when its conditions were read out both Major Byles and the Rev. Septimus Cunliffe objected to it, though on totally different grounds, and urged that Leonard should be asked to substitute something else. However, on a vote being taken, it was agreed by a considerable majority that "The Kiss Problem" should be retained, although, as the chairman pointed out, it looked excessively dangerous.

Mr. Pusely-Smythe was reminded that it was his turn to be chairman at the next meeting. And then, the business of the evening being at an end, the card-tables were brought in, and members addressed themselves to bridge at moderate points.

No. II
The Kiss Problem

Mr. Pusely-Smythe's air of saturnine melancholy was pronounced as he took the chair at the forty-fourth monthly meeting of the Problem Club.

"Well, gentlemen," he began, "the waiters are supposed to have left the room, but in view of the nature of the problem before us to-night you would probably wish to be quite sure on the point. Will somebody kindly examine the screen by the waiters' entrance?"

Mr. Quillian, K.C., reported that no waiter was concealed, and further that the door was locked.

"Thank you, my learned friend. Leonard—admirable as a head-waiter, ingenious and generally innocuous as the inventor of our problems—has on this occasion undergone a moral lapse. I will give you the words of this lamentable problem: 'It is required within the space of one hour to kiss upon the cheek ten females of the age of courtship and not cousins or any nearer relative of the kisser, without giving offence to any one of them.'

"Major Byles protested against this problem on the ground that it gave an unfair advantage to the young and unattached. The Rev. Septimus Cunliffe seconded the protest on the ground that, broad-minded though he was, after all there was a limit. A vote being taken, it was found—to the eternal shame of the club, if I may say so—that there was a considerable majority in favour of the problem being retained."

Every member being well aware that the chairman himself had voted with the majority, there was some hilarious interruption.

"Gentlemen," said the chairman severely, "this is not the spirit in which to approach stories of wrecked homes and blasted reputations, and these stories we must now hear. I observe that Mr. Quillian has had his face scratched recently, doubtless the work of outraged modesty, but before I—"

"I really must protest," said Mr. Quillian. "The slight marks on my left cheek are not scratches, but were caused—as they say at the inquests—by some blunt instrument, to wit, a safety razor."

"Well," the chairman continued, "you will have an opportunity later to explain how the girl got hold of the razor. I will begin with some of our younger Lotharios. What have you to tell us, Mr. Feldane?"

The Hon. James Feldane put down his cigarette, and spoke wearily: "It's like this, you know. I claim to have won unless my score's beaten. Ten in an hour is an impossible demand on the part of our friend Leonard, and I doubt if bogey would be more than four. May I take it that I win, if I am nearest to Leonard's figure?"

"That is so. Continue your loathsome confessions."

"It's strictly masonic and all that, ain't it?"

"Mr. Feldane may be assured that his hideous secret will die with us," said the chairman. "The club rule of secrecy has never yet been broken."

"That being so, I'll get on. I'd planned it all for a dance I was going to, and I'd put in a deal of conscientious preliminary work, getting certain girls up to a certain mark, if you understand what I mean. On the appointed night a perfectly dear old thing with two daughters some years older than myself called to take me on to that dance. They've known me all my life. They knew me when I'd got golden curls and played with a wool rabbit. They're no sort of relation, and so they count for the purpose of this competition. Well, I've always kissed them when we met, and I kissed them that time as soon as I boarded the car. So when we got to the house where the dance was I was three up and still had fifty-three minutes to go."

Here Feldane was interrupted by an appeal to the chairman. It was made by his friend Hesseltine, a tall and dark young man, as good-looking as Feldane himself, though of a very different type.

"Mr. Chairman," said Hesseltine, "before Jimmy goes any further I should like to ask for your ruling. The mother of those two girls is to my certain knowledge sixty-two years of age. I claim that Jimmy cannot score her, as she is above the age of courtship."

"Sorry, Mr. Hesseltine, but your claim is disallowed. It has been well observed that a man is as old as he feels, but that a woman is rather younger than she doesn't look. There is no historical instance of any woman being over the age of courtship."

"Then I'm pipped," said Hesseltine gloomily. "Go on, Jimmy."

"I kissed four more in the time left me, but one of them told me that she would never speak to me again, and so I can't count her, though it's what she always says. I was done by the time limit. You can't in decency kiss a girl and then do an immediate bunk. You must keep on telling her how maddeningly beautiful she is for a few minutes. Besides, at a dance you can't always find the girl you want at the moment you want her. Still, I claim a score of six."

"The claim is allowed. And what was your sad experience, Mr. Hesseltine?"

"Much the same as Jimmy's. I went to the same dance. I also played the friends-of-my-childhood, but I could only raise five of them. So Jimmy's one ahead. If you had disallowed his old lady we should have tied. I might add that, being rather carried away, I got engaged to two different girls in the course of the hour, and though it's all right now, I don't monkey with a buzzsaw again. The next kiss problem will find little Bobby seated with the spectators."

"Possibly," said the chairman, "the finesse and experience of riper years will have accomplished more than the attractions of untutored youth. May I interrupt your secretarial duties, Sir Charles?"

Sir Charles laid down his pencil, smiled, and shook his head. "This time you must place me also with the spectators," he said, and quoted an apt line of Horace.

"It is seldom that you miss. I wish Mr. Harding Pope, that I could say the same of you. What have you done this time to redeem yourself?"

"What could I do?" said Mr. Pope, with an oratorical gesture. "I represent a Nonconformist constituency which is not tolerant of the least laxity in the private life of its member. The mere suspicion that I had taken part in a competition of this kind might end my political career."

"Possibly. Failure to take part in the next competition will actually end your career as a member of this club, as you will see if you refer to rule eleven. The club does not regard onlookers as sportsmen. I suppose, Major Byles, since you protested against the problem, that for the first time in your membership you have failed to compete."

"That is so, but my protest had very little to do with it. Matter of fact, I had a superstitious idea that it might change my luck if I gave a miss this time."

"Then I will turn to Dr. Alden. What was your adventure, doctor?"

"Mine was more a tragedy than an adventure," said the doctor. "On the evening of Sunday the twelfth, acting on information received, I presented myself at the residence of my married sister. She said that I must have forgotten that she was entertaining the girls of her Tennyson Club that night, and that she had never wanted me less, but that, as I was there, I could stop. I stopped, that being what I had come for. Her suggestion that her husband and myself, the only two males present, should go off to the billiard-room after supper, was negatived by both of us. In accordance with plan I then directed the conversation to the subject of face-powder, condemning it on scientific grounds and maintaining that it deceived nobody. My sister said that it was not intended to deceive, but that as a matter of fact no man would ever detect it unless it had been put on with a shovel. I said that, on the contrary, given a certain condition, any man with a scientific training could detect it with his eyes shut.

"Several of the girls asked me how. This was not unexpected.

"I replied that he would only have to touch with his lips a cheek on which there was face-powder and he would know it instantly and infallibly.

"My sister said she did not believe a word of it.

"My answer was that I could easily prove it. Let them blindfold me. Then twelve times in succession let a cheek touch my lips. In each case I would state whether or not face-powder had been used, and would employ no other means of detection. I was so certain of it that I would gladly contribute a guinea to the charitable fund of the Tennyson Club for every mistake that I made.

"My sister said that it was very easy to make an impossible offer that could not be accepted. Somewhat to my surprise the prettiest girl there said that she did not think it an impossible offer at all. It was a scientific experiment and might benefit a very good cause. I would never know the identity of the twelve who took part in the experiment. Its very publicity made it innocuous. But I should have to give them a little time to settle which were the twelve to be sacrificed and the order in which they were to present themselves. To this I at once agreed.

"I was put in a chair and blindfolded—really blindfolded. I need hardly tell the members of this club that my claim to be able to detect the presence of face-powder in the way indicated was a piece of monumental spoof. This did not alarm me. I could not lose more than twelve guineas, and I was out to win our prize of one hundred and ten pounds. I could assign my mistakes to the fact that I had just smoked a cigarette, thus spoiling the delicacy of my perception.

"I heard a sound of whispering and suppressed laughter as the girls held their consultation, and then the experiment began in silence, broken only by the rustle of feminine garments. Twelve times in succession I felt a gentle touch upon my lips, and never once did I fail to take advantage of it. I gave six decisions for face-powder and six against, and was just thinking how I would spend the hundred and ten pounds when I heard a roar of laughter. I tore off the bandage and asked what was the matter.

"As soon as they could speak they told me. The only person that I had kissed on all twelve occasions was my own sister. Sometimes she had touched my lips with her cheek, on which there was face-powder, and sometimes with the back of her hand, on which there was none. And nine times I had been mistaken in my diagnosis. The treasurer of the charitable fund—she was the pretty girl of whom I have spoken—collected the money. Then they all resumed their merriment, and no excuse for my mistakes was ever heard.

"All things considered, I think I have a fair claim for a consolation prize."

"The club does not give prizes of that description," said the chairman. "But I can offer you our sympathy, which is more valuable than mere money. I will now call upon Mr. Quillian."

Mr. Quillian adjusted his pince-nez. "I will ask the chairman's permission to argue that the whole of this competition is null and void, and that the prize should be added to that for the next competition."

"I will hear you, Mr. Quillian, but you must be brief and to the point. You are not in court now, you know."

"If you please, I submit that a kiss has a psychical as well as a physical side, and that kisses for competition purposes are so deficient on the psychical or emotional side that they cannot be considered as kisses in the ordinary sense of the word."

"I do not admit that. Possibly the competition kiss does not come up to the standard demanded by a voluptuary like my learned friend, but it is still a kiss. If he kissed this match-box, it would be a kiss and could not be described otherwise, although presumably the emotional side would be absent. Enough of these legal quibbles. I will now ask Mr. Matthews if he has been as successful in the part of Lothario as he invariably is in that of Lucullus."

Mr. Matthews, the club epicure, said that a decent upbringing had caused him to fail in a shameful enterprise, and gave his account of it.

He advertised in the name of Mrs. Elsmere Twiss, giving an accommodation address, for a companion to an elderly lady. The salary offered was magnificent, and it was intimated that accomplishments would be less valued than youthful charm and an affectionate nature. Applicants were to enclose photographs.

Ten of the applicants—and it is to be feared that they were the ten whose photographs were the most attractive—were given an appointment with Mrs. Elsmere Twiss at a West End hotel on a certain day. On the morning of that day Mr. Matthews placed himself in the hands of a famous costumier, who had guaranteed to convert him into such an excellent imitation of an old lady that even at close quarters the disguise would not be detected. The costumier spent two hours on effecting a most artistic transformation and then, after submitting himself to the photographer in attendance, Mr. Matthew drove off to the hotel. A passer-by who had happened to glance into the cab might have observed a sweet-looking old lady smoking a large cigar.

He now proceeded to interview the selected ten, it being his abominable intention to kiss each applicant as he said good-bye to her.

The first applicant to be brought in from the waiting-room was Miss Grace Porter. Everything went well until the moment came for the affectionate good-bye. But then it chanced that Miss Porter dropped her handkerchief.

Now Mr. Matthews had from the nursery upwards been taught habits of politeness, and his decent upbringing now proved his undoing. Forgetting that he was supposed to be an elderly lady and the girl's prospective employer, he flew to pick up that handkerchief. And as he stooped his hat and wig fell off. For a few awful moments he remained stooping, waiting for Miss Porter's scream. But no scream came. She had realised that Mrs. Elsmere Twiss wore a wig, but not that she was a man. And the tactful Miss Porter had retired from the room.

Mr. Matthews was safe, but his nerve was gone. He replaced the hat and wig, and sent a waiter with a message to the remaining applicants.

When Mr. Matthews had finished his story two other members narrated how they had conspired together to get the game of kiss-in-the-ring played at a rectory garden party and had failed miserably.

"Now the only member left," said the chairman, "is Mr. Cunliffe, and as he protested against the problem, and will not have competed—"

"Pardon me," said the sonorous and ecclesiastical voice of the Rev. Septimus Cunliffe. "I have not only competed, but I claim to be the winner."

"One moment. This is a shock, and some restorative seems indicated." The chairman fetched himself a brandy-and-soda from the side-table and resumed. "Now, if the reverend gentleman will continue the account of his exploits—"

"It has pained me to hear to-night aspersions on the character of our admirable Leonard. I admit that when I first heard the problem I was myself inclined to misjudge him. But on examining it more closely I saw that never had he risen to a higher pitch of austere, though cynical, morality. I saw that he intended that this prize should be won by the most high-minded member of the club—by the man whose mind was the least obsessed by thoughts of frivolity or flirtation."

"Might I suggest," said the chairman, "that you should stop throwing bouquets to yourself, and tell us about these ten women that you've kissed?"

"That is precisely my point. Leonard does not say women. He does not say girls. He says females. My aunt is interested in smoke-gray Persian cats. She breeds them and deals in them on behalf of a charity, and you will generally find thirty or forty of them at her house. It is unhygienic to kiss, cats, but I kissed ten of them, and my aunt was greatly pleased at this unusual demonstration of affection for her pets. Some of them seemed slightly bored, but not one was offended. When a cat is offended it tells you so. They were of an age for courtship—by males of their own species. Briefly, the cats and I conformed in all respects with the requirements of the problem."

"Gentlemen," said the chairman, "the subtlety of our theologian has overcome you. Our cheque for one hundred and ten pounds will be drawn to the order of Mr. Septimus Cunliffe.

"I will now read out the problem which will next engage your attention. It is entitled 'The Free Meal Problem.' It is required within the space of twenty-four consecutive hours to be the guest of one person at breakfast, of another at luncheon, and of a third at dinner, the host being in each case a person whom the competitor has not to his knowledge seen, and with whom he has held no communication previous to the sunrise preceding the meal. No direct request for a meal may be made and no remuneration may be given in return for any meal.

"The adjudicator will be my learned friend Mr. Quillian."

No. III
The Free Meal Problem

Probably no member of the Problem Club enjoyed his evening of chairmanship more than Mr. Quillian, K.C., who occupied the chair at the forty-fifth meeting. He liked the position of authority, and he liked the opportunity to exercise the nicety and precision of his legal mind. In the Free Meal Problem, on which he was to adjudicate, the ingenious head-waiter Leonard had made the following demand:—

"It is required within the space of twenty-four consecutive hours to be the guest of one person at breakfast, of another at luncheon, and of a third at dinner, the host being in each case a person whom the competitor has not to his knowledge seen, and with whom he has held no communication, previous to the sunrise preceding the meal. No direct request for a meal may be made, and no remuneration may be given in return for any meal."

"Now, gentlemen," said Mr. Quillian, when he had read this out, "this is a problem where the question of definition may arise. For instance, a child in a railway carriage offers a traveler a small piece of deteriorated bun. We will suppose that the hour is eight in the morning and that the traveler has not partaken of food since the previous midnight. In the improbable event of his consuming the—er—proffered dainty, he has undoubtedly broken his fast. But can he be said to have breakfasted? All I can say is that if the question of definition should arise to-night I will do my best to deal with it on commonsense lines, accurately but without pedantry."

The chairman then called upon Mr. Wildersley, A.R.A., to give his experiences.

Wildersley was a man of middle age who, like many artists, retained something of the child in his composition. He was a big, good-tempered man of rather rugged appearance. The cigars provided by the club, good though they were, had no attraction for him. He was a pipe-smoker, and between his sentences he contrived to keep his pipe alight.

"Well," he said, "I mayn't be a winner, but I can't be far out. I'll tell you how I set about it. You may have noticed that chaps in the country with little places—three or four acres—are often very keen about them. In fact, the smaller the place the keener they are. My frame-maker, who lives near Harrow, used to spend most of his Sunday afternoon sitting behind a curtain with the window open, listening to what passers-by had to say about the godetias in his front garden. His daughter sometimes sits for me, and she told me that if the compliments on the garden came in nicely it put him in such a good temper that he used to let the family off church in the evening. I decided to work on the pride that the owner or tenant has in his place. I went down to the outer suburban belt—the part that they call the real country—and put up at an hotel. Then bright and early one morning I started out with my painting contraptions. I very soon spotted a place that I knew must be picturesque, be-cause it had got some clipped yews and a sun-dial; besides, as the gate informed me, it was called the Dream House, and that proved it. So in I went, pitched my easel half-way up the drive, and got to work. An old gardener came up and asked me if I knew that I was trespassing. So I gave him a shilling, my card, and my apologies. I told him to keep the shilling and to deliver the card and apologies to his master as soon as that gentleman got down. That seemed to meet the case. In half an hour I had knocked off something showy, and then down the drive towards me came the owner, all smiles and Norfolk jacket, with a Cocker spaniel trailing behind him. I gave him the sketch, and he was as pleased as Punch about it. He took me round the garden to point out other picturesque spots, and then brought me into the house to introduce me to his family. Nice people, very. Almost before I knew it I was breakfast-ing with them, and being hungry I was pleased to find that they took breakfast seriously. They'd have kept me there all day if I could have stopped, but the business of this problem required me to move on.

"At half-past twelve I played the same trick again six miles up the road. Once more it worked perfectly. My hostess was an old lady of the almost extinct type that knows how to live. Everything about the place was just exactly. The luncheon was just exactly. And she gave me a very fine old Amontillado—a wine that we don't see enough of nowadays. I can't say whether it was the sherry or the success, but when I left I felt that I had got the club's cheque for one hundred and ten pounds in my pocket and was listening to the chairman's kindly words of congratulation. My mistake, of course. Begin well, but not too well. If you begin too well, mistrust it.

"About seven that evening I was painting a garden which was really rather good in that light. (I'd sent in my card and got permission.) As I was finishing the job and rather wrapped up in it I heard a Scotch accent behind me, saying that the sketch was 'no bad' and 'verra like.' He and I discussed the comparative merits of painting and photography. For accuracy he 'prefaired the photograph, but then it didna give the colours.' As before, I presented the sketch, and I still think that he was pleased with it. He asked me to sign it, so as to prove to his friends that he 'wasna lying' when he said that it was by a professed painter, and admitted that he would not grudge the money it would cost for framing and glazing. He then said he made no doubt I would be hurrying home for my dinner, and he would wish me good-evening. And so, in a manner of speaking, I fell at the last hurdle. Still, I suppose I score the breakfast and luncheon."

The Hon. James Feldane addressed the chairman:—

"I'd like your ruling on that point, sir. And it's quite impartial, because I am not competing myself this time."

"Not competing?" said the chairman. "Might I ask what stopped you? Hitherto you have been one of the keenest and most sporting of our members, in spite of your air of—er—lassitude."

"What stopped me," said Jimmy simply, "was breakfast. Breakfast is bad enough at any time, especially if you've been rather late

and busy the night before. But to breakfast with an absolute
stranger on chance food, and to go out and dig for the invitation
first—well, it was unthinkable. I'm sorry to spoil old Wildersley's
score, and if he'd bunged me one of his sketches instead of chuck-
ing them about the suburbs I might have been able to stifle the
voice of conscience. As it is, I feel bound to raise the objection that
he gave remuneration for the breakfast and luncheon—to wit, two
sketches."

"The gift of the sketches was precedent to the meals and was
unconditional, as we see by the fact that the third sketch produced
no meal. The sketches were a lure, and the use of a lure is not prohibited. They were not remuneration given in return for a meal. I
should not even say that the meals were remuneration for the
sketches; they were merely an expression of gratitude. Mr. Feldane's objection is disallowed."

That habitual non-starter Mr. Harding Pope, M.P., was now asked
if he had made his choice between competition or resignation.

"I have competed, of course. But I have only the most dismal
of failures to record. I was down at my constituency, and I picked
out three new residents on whom I had a plausible excuse for calling. I 'phoned the first to ask if he could see me at nine, apologising
for the earliness of the hour. He said that the time suited him very
well, and that, as a matter of fact, he always breakfasted at seven,
so as to begin work early. The man whom I called on at lunch-time
could only give me ten minutes, he said, as he was lunching out.
The third did ask me to dinner, but not on that day. And probably
all three have put me down as a man who calls at tactless and in-
convenient times. I can only say that I am ready to suffer far worse
things for the privilege of retaining my membership."

Sir Charles Bunford had perhaps shown rather more strategy,
but had only one degree less of failure to report. He had obtained
letters of introduction to three noted food-cranks, all of them
ardent proselytisers. To the first he represented himself as suffering from a list of symptoms. Sir Charles had memorised them carefully from the advertisement of a patent pill. He said that he
was sorry to call at so early an hour, but after a night of suffering

he had determined that he would begin on a new system of diet at once.

"For instance," he said, "what ought I to have for breakfast this morning? What do you have yourself?"

The food-crank said that he would not only tell him; he would ask him to share his simple but healthful fare.

At this point in his narrative the chairman interposed.

"This is a case where the question of definition may arise. I must ask you to tell us, Sir Charles, what the food-crank gave you for breakfast."

"It was not so much breakfast as a premature dessert with a hospital flavour to it. It consisted of uncooked fruit and lessons in the difficult art of mastication. With that we drank a special sort of coffee, from which all deleterious matter, including the taste of coffee, had been entirely removed. But the question of definition need not worry you, as I can't claim to have won. The second food crank, whom I visited at lunch-time, told me that his chief secret was never to eat in the middle of the day. The third, whom I tackled in the evening, was so ascetic in his conversation and so extremely anxious to keep me out of his dining-room, that I formed a suspicion, perhaps unworthy, that the man's practice differed somewhat from his preaching. So I've failed, but it was quite an amusing day."

That great epicure, Mr. Matthews, had not competed, and gave his reasons with a solemnity that contrasted with his usual cheeriness.

"Thank Heaven," he said, "I have a sophisticated appetite! Thank Heaven again I have an over-educated palate! Starvation for twenty-four hours I might have possibly faced. But the horrors of casual hospitality were more than I could risk."

"Ah, well," said the chairman, "I must turn to Mr. Pusely-Smythe, who is acting as secretary for us to-night. I presume he has added one more to his list of triumphs."

"The pangs of failure," said that saturnine gentleman, "are increased by the jeers of the learned chairman. I ought to have won. I claim to have won. But I confess that it will not surprise me if I

am reduced to an equality with my artist friend. I shall have a
melancholy pleasure in sharing the prize with him. He tried to work
upon gratitude, and so did I. The particular brand of gratitude that
I decided to exploit for my purpose was the gratitude that a woman
feels for the return of her lost pet dog. It seems to vary inversely
as the value of the dog, but it is always great.

"You will perhaps remember that about a year ago Leonard set
us a peculiarly sinful problem, which he styled the Substitution
Problem, and that in the complicated and unjustifiable operations
by which I succeeded in winning the prize I made the acquaintance
of James Tigg, and did him a good turn. Now James, known to his
intimate friends as 'Kidney,' is by profession a French polisher,
but does not practice, and his favourite occupation is the appro-
priation of dogs, his gifts in that direction amounting almost to
genius.

"I sent for James. I told him that I thought it likely that three
ladies, living in different suburbs, would lose their pet dogs and
that I should know where to find them, and should be enabled by
the address on the dog-collar to return each of the little darlings
to its owner. At the same time I put five golden sovereigns on the
table.

"'Likely?' said James. 'It's a ruddy certainty.' He then picked
up the coins in an absent-minded way and instructed me as to details.

"Two days later, at an early hour in the morning, I called on
Lady Pingle at her house at Epsom with her ladyship's alleged
Pekingese under my arm. I told her how I had found the poor little
thing wandering on Wimbledon Common late the night before almost in a state of collapse, had given it food and shelter, and had
taken the earliest opportunity to relieve her anxiety by its return.

"Her gratitude was almost frantic. She kissed the dog ardently,
and at one moment I was almost afraid she was going to kiss me
too. She did not do that, but she did insist on my breakfasting with
her, and I accepted. And let me tell that over-educated sybarite
Matthews, with his sneers at casual hospitality, that he himself
never breakfasted better.

"I lunched with Mrs. Hastonbury at her residence at Leatherhead. In this way she showed her gratitude for the return of 'Bimby'—a chocolate-coloured Pom with a short temper. But I must confess that she was not nearly as quick off the mark as Lady Pingle. I had to inquire about hotels in the neighbourhood before she saw which way her duty lay.

"The third dog that I had to deliver, a mouldy little pug, belonged to the wife of a curate living much nearer home. She was grateful and she was hospitable. She said that they never dined but that they were just sitting down to high tea, and she hoped I would join them. It was an evening meal substituted for dinner, and I contend that I am entitled to count it as dinner."

"Kindly tell us what you had," said the chairman.

"What? The internal evidence? Certainly. I had cocoa, scrambled eggs, and seed-cake. And I hope you will take a lenient view of it."

"Your hostess herself maintained that it was not dinner, and the internal evidence, as you call it, entirely supports her view. Your career of crime will only give you a score of two. The high tea is disallowed. I will now call upon Major Byles."

"The sacrifice that I made to luck on the occasion of our last competition," said Major Byles, "has brought me success at last. I claim to be a winner, and await your decision with confidence. It happened that two of my friends both wanted a furnished house at Brightgate for the winter, and did not want the bother of going down to make their selection. I saw my chance at once. I might never have thought of it, but I didn't miss it when it was shoved at me. I said at once that I was thinking of running down to Brightgate for a day or two, and that it always interested me to look over houses. They told me their requirements and let me take on the job for them.

"The house-agent at Brightgate had only six houses on his books that were at all suitable. He gave me orders to view, and I started business at eight one morning. I started badly.

"At the first house a proud but pretty parlour-maid told me that it was not usual to show furnished houses at that hour, but I could

call again at eleven. At the second house there was only a caretaker. That left me with, so to speak, four cartridges and three birds
to kill. I hurried on to the third house, which was half a mile away.
By a bit of luck I met the owner on the doorstep, and told him my
alleged business.

"'You're very early,' he said. 'Why, we haven't had breakfast yet.'

"'No more have I,' I said. 'But last year I lost a good house
through being too late, and I thought I wouldn't make the same
mistake again.'

"He was a genial old chap. He said the best thing I could do
was to come in and breakfast with him, and by the time I had finished the servants would have got the bedrooms tidied up. I did
my best to accept with decent hesitation.

"At lunch-time I tried the fourth house on my list and struck
another caretaker. I couldn't afford another miss. I got lunch at
the fifth house, but I had to be no end complimentary before I could
get them up to the point. In fact, it wasn't till I told the woman
that her pimply-faced son was a fine upstanding young fellow that
she decided to order the extra chop.

"But at the sixth house I had no trouble about dinner. The owner
turned out to be a friend of a friend of mine. He fetched up a bottle
of the '87 in my honour and insisted on my stopping the night.

"They were all *pukka* meals, and all the conditions were observed. Am I a winner, Mr. Chairman?"

"Certainly. Does anybody else claim to be a winner?"

"I do," said Dr. Alden. "The day before yesterday a doctor rang
me up and asked me to see a patient of his—a woman with a
wealthy, devoted, and very nervous husband. That was at eight in
the morning. My car happened to be at the door, and it suited me
to go right away. I saw the patient, was able to reassure the husband, and had breakfast with him. Later in the morning a man was
introduced to me who was interested in old glass and had heard of
me as a collector. He was very keen that I should lunch with him
and see what he had got. He was a pleasant chap and I accepted.
When I got back, a doctor, quite an old pal of mine, said that he
was going to take me to dine that night with a man I had never

seen before. It seemed that the stranger had staying with him for one night a French specialist in my own line. The Frenchman was anxious to meet me, and his host was anxious to please him. So he had tried to arrange it through a mutual friend. I was myself keen to meet that Frenchman, and so he succeeded.

"Of course, I didn't arrange all this—couldn't have arranged it. As a matter of fact, I had never intended to compete this time. But destiny decided to take a hand in this competition. I claim to be a winner."

"An interesting point," said the chairman. "Can a man be said to win who has never competed? I shall decide in Dr. Alden's favour. Leonard says nothing of intention. He only demands certain facts. And these facts the doctor by an amazing stroke of luck has been able to provide. The prize of one hundred and ten pounds will be divided equally between him and Major Byles, unless there is any further claim."

No further claim was forthcoming. The chairman then announced that Mr. Matthews would preside at the next meeting, and read out the problem set for the following month, called "The Win-and-Lose Problem," and there was a general feeling that it would take some doing.

No. IV
The Win-and-Lose Problem

At the forty-sixth meeting of the Problem Club, the waiters having left the room, Mr. Matthews, smiling and rubicund, took his place as chairman. He finished his glass of an old and veritable cognac, lit with care and a cedar-wood spill a cigar that can only be obtained by the favour of the planter, and read out the terms of the Win-and-Lose Problem.

"It is required to win an even bet of one pound, resulting in a net loss of one pound to the winner; and to lose an even bet of one pound resulting in a net gain of one pound to the loser. No competitor is to make more than two bets."

"Well, gentlemen," said Mr. Matthews, "I'm supposed to make one or two preliminary observations. Now here's a thing that strikes me. You may remember that when we tackled the Kiss Problem, our reverend friend Mr. Cunliffe said that it revealed the artful Leonard as an apostle of morality. Of course, the padre took the jack-pot on that occasion, and so he may have been prejudiced, but it looks to me now as if he may have been right. See for yourselves. You've got to win a bet and lose money by it, and then you've got to lose a bet and make money by it, and at the end of it you're left just where you were when you started. There's not much deadly fascination and excitement about that—why, it's enough to make you lose your taste for gambling.

"Yes, and there's one more point. I noticed a good deal of preoccupation at dinner to-night. Very few of you seemed to be putting your heart into the work, and I believe I was the only man who had the *vol-au-vent* brought back to him for further reference. Great mistake that of yours. Some of you tried to work out sums on the back of your menus. I detected Major Byles, with corrugated brows, in the act of making pencil calculations on the tablecloth. Yes, there's not a doubt that Leonard has given you a worrying time, and some of you were wrestling with it right up to the last moment. It won't surprise me if there's not a winner among the whole lot of you. However, we'll begin with a likely chance. You, Sir Charles, have got a reputation as a learned man; can I ask the secretary to draw a cheque in your favour?"

"I'd be sorry to stop you," said Sir Charles, "but I'm afraid I can't claim it. Archaeology don't help with arithmetic. As an eminent classical scholar once observed, I've not got the low cunning that makes a mathematician. The only thing I could think of was to insure the chances of each bet appropriately, but it seemed to me that you would regard such insurance as being in itself a bet."

"I certainly should. You don't change a thing by changing its name. You are limited to the two bets, and I shall not allow four even if you call two of them insurance. Come now, Jimmy, have you profited sufficiently by your racing experiences to have won the prize to-night?"

"Profited by my racing experiences?" said the Hon. James Feldane wearily. "If you'd go and talk to the bank that has charge of my overdraft you wouldn't use words like those. But backing horses, though it's a mug's game, is, at any rate, easy. There are too many complications in Leonard's fancy work for a simple child of Nature like myself. I can't engineer a two-cylinder gamble with a double back-jump actuated by the camshaft. The only man I know who could face it without mental overstrain is my bookmaker. He's a wonder. He'd give you fifteen different ways of perforating this problem inside a minute. No juggle with figures can beat him. I don't know if you'd call it a talent or a disease, but I've not got it. As a competitor, I've failed, but I don't mind admitting that I've made a little actual money out of the competition." Jimmy smiled reminiscently.

"May we have the details?" asked the chairman.

"I'd sooner you got them from Hesseltine."

The chairman called upon Mr. Hesseltine.

"I don't wonder," said that young man, "that Jimmy don't like to tell you. If *I'd* stolen money from a crossing-sweeper in St James's Street I shouldn't be proud of it myself. The silly ass thinks he's scored off me, but as I was out to lose a quid anyhow—"

"May we have the actual facts?" suggested the chairman.

"Certainly. I was thinking about this problem and I got a sudden brain-wave. I saw how to do the first half—to win a bet of a pound that would leave me one pound down when I'd won it. Well, I happened to be going up St James's Street with Jimmy later that morning, and by way of leading up to it I asked him what he generally gave to a street-beggar. 'Nix,' he said. 'What do you?' So I told him that I generally gave a sovereign. He told me in his coarse sort of way that he didn't believe it. That was what I had expected. 'All right,' I said, 'I'll bet you a pound that I give two golden sovereigns to the next beggar or crossing-sweeper I come across.' He thought about it and then said: 'I'll take that, and to guard against accidents I'll be the next beggar. Give me a little assistance, kind sir?'

"Of course, in that way he put himself on velvet. Whether I decided to win my bet or to lose it, Jimmy had to make one sovereign out of me. Didn't affect me at all, for according to Leonard I'd got to win my bet and lose a pound by it, which I did. The only person hit was the crossing-sweeper up the street, who would otherwise have made two quid. Of course, what I ought to have done was to have handed Jimmy over to the police for begging—wish I'd thought of it.

"Well, I negotiated the first half of the problem, but the second half beat me. I'm inclined to think the sting of the beast is in its tail. It takes two people to make a bet. I'm not a poet or any sort of imaginative chap, but I could think of a bet which for a dead certainty it would pay me to lose. I couldn't think of anybody, even including that rotter Jimmy, who would be fool enough to take it. You must try somebody else, Mr. Chairman."

"Major Byles?" the chairman suggested.

"As a head-waiter," said the Major, "I've got nothing against Leonard. As a setter of problems he's given general satisfaction, but this time I should like to back my bill to the effect that he has mixed up too much arithmetic with the sport. I've spent a month on this win-and-lose business, all the time with the feeling that a boy fresh from school would work out the whole thing on the back of an envelope in ten minutes, and I've done nothing. I spent the first fortnight at home, and at the end of it I had contracted insomnia, headache, and what you might call pardonable irritability. At the end of that time my wife said that of course she had noticed the change, and that I seemed to be doing sums all day, and that if we were ruined I had better say so and she would face it bravely. I reassured her and came to town on important business. I used tons of the club notepaper for my calculations, put an undue strain on the club wastepaper-baskets, quarreled with two of my best friends, was sarcastic in addressing club servants, and am expecting a letter from the committee to ask for my resignation. The amazing thing is that all the time I have been on the very point of getting the solution. In my opinion it's the most horribly worrying thing that Leonard has ever given us."

"Well," said the chairman, "artists are not generally supposed to be particularly strong at arithmetic, but I'll ask Mr. Wildersley what he's done about it."

"Can't say I agree with the Major," said Wildersley. "I call it a jolly easy problem, and I claim to be a winner. It didn't take me any time to think of it, either. I got a man into my studio, to see alleged works of art, and I said to him that I would bet him a pound I would give him two pounds. He took me. 'You've lost,' I said. 'Pay up, and then I'll pay up.' He handed me a sovereign and I handed him two pounds of potatoes in a paper bag. So I'd won a pound in money and lost two pounds in potatoes. If you win one pound and lose two, that makes a net loss of one pound on the transaction, and so I'd done the first half of the problem.

"The chap seemed to be grumbling rather. 'What's the matter with you?' I said. 'The green-grocer told me that they were the kind he eats himself, and that he could guarantee them.'

"'I don't want the beastly potatoes,' he said. 'The whole thing's a dirty swindle.' I thought he'd say that. So I told him that it was no swindle and I would be quite willing to take the same bet myself. He jumped at it, but to make sure he said he would bet me a sovereign he would give me two pounds. I took him, lost, paid the sovereign, and got back my two pounds of potatoes. That finished the second half of the problem. I'd lost a bet of one pound, and had made two pounds, giving a net gain of one pound. Naturally he wanted to know what I had done it for, and I said it was to stop him from trying to talk about art—the chap's a critic."

Mr. Matthews took two minutes and a brandy-and-soda before giving his decision as follows:—

"Ingenious, but it won't do. Mr. Wildersley professes to have subtracted money to the value of a sovereign from two pounds by weight of potatoes, and to have got a result of one pound. Of what did that pound consist? Even after dinner we can't have mental confusion of this kind. The claim is disallowed."

Mr. Harding Pope, M.P., made an uninteresting confession of failure, and the chairman then called upon Mr. Quillian, K.C., who was acting as secretary for the evening.

Mr. Quillian removed his pince-nez and glanced round the room with that look of amiable superiority that some people found irritating.

"I claim to have won this fairly simple competition," he said. "Of course, it has a psychological as well as an arithmetical side; the bets have to be actually made and not merely worked out on paper. I made my plan one afternoon, and then went over to my club to see if I could find my friend Blenkinsop. He is generally at the club at that hour, and I felt sure that he would accept the two bets that I had to propose.

"Well, as it happened, Blenkinsop was not at the club, but I found Mr. Pusely-Smythe alone in the smaller reading-room. I've had to submit to a good deal of chaff—not particularly amusing— from Pusely-Smythe, and by way of return it seemed appropriate that he should help me to win our one hundred and ten pound prize. Also, if he will forgive me for saying so, he has just the commonplace shrewdness that I required in my victim.

"After a little preliminary conversation, I produced my sovereign-case. I told him that there was a certain sum of money in gold in that case, and that I was willing to bet him a sovereign I would make him a present of it. He said, as I knew he would, that this meant that the sum of money in the case was half a sovereign, and that in consequence he would lose ten shillings on the transaction if he took the bet.

"'Yes,' I said, 'there is that possibility, but I am willing to protect you against it by a second bet. We will agree that the loser by the first transaction shall have the option to give the other man double what he has lost for double the sum now in my sovereign-case. And I will bet you a sovereign that he will not exercise that option. You see how it works out. If the sum in my sovereign-case is half a sovereign, as you suppose, you will lose ten shillings on the first transaction, but you will win a sovereign on the second transaction by exercising an option to exchange twenty shillings for twenty shillings.'

"Without taking the time to think, he accepted both bets. I then opened my sovereign-case and showed him that it contained two pounds. I gave them to him, and as by so doing I had won my bet he gave me one of them back again. Kindly observe that I had now solved the first part of Leonard's problem. I had won an even bet of one pound the net result of which was that I had lost a pound. Having made myself the loser on the first transaction, I now had the option to exchange twice my loss against twice the sum that had been in the sovereign case—that is, to exchange two pounds for four pounds. I had bet that the loser would not exercise this option. I lost the bet and exercised the option. Thus, I lost an even bet of one pound with the net result that I made one pound. This settles the second half of the problem. I await, sir, with confidence, your decision in my favour."

Mr. Matthews referred once more to the terms of the problem. "Yes," he said, "it seems to me that you have met all Leonard's requirements. Very smart bit of work, in my opinion. You take the club cheque for one hundred and ten pounds, unless, of course, some claim to share it with you is substantiated. Is there any such claim?"

"Naturally, there's mine," said Pusely-Smythe, with his deceptive air of melancholy.

"Yours? How did you do it?"

"My learned friend has just been telling you. I was going away for a brief and well-earned holiday, and I had decided to give the competition a miss this time. As I was sitting in the club, studying a guide-book, in came Quillian looking like a thimble-rigger who has just set up his little plush-covered table. He offered me his first bet. I put it aside. He offered the second, and he says I didn't take time to think. Thought with me does not take the prolonged period of gestation that it does in the case of the nobler animals, such as K.C.'s. I thought two thoughts. The first was that Quillian was out after this competition. The second was that when two men gamble together what one wins the other loses and vice versa. That was enough. I took him. He won the first bet but lost a pound by it. It follows that I lost the first bet but won a pound by it. Similarly, when he lost the bet but won a pound I won the bet and lost a pound. It's all very simple and elementary. I hope he's going to make a victim of me again soon. This time without any effort on my part he has shoved fifty-five pounds at me. I've only had to take it. And I don't care whether it was benevolence or mental shortsightedness—I'm going to thank him just the same."

"The claim's allowed, of course," said the chairman. "The thing that makes me mad is that I didn't see it myself until you pointed it out. It's obvious. It simply shrieks at you. My mind must be going."

"The menu that you devised for our dinner to-night, sir," said Pusely-Smythe, "was sufficient proof of the contrary. Those that study the recondite must sometimes find the obvious out of their focus."

"Thank you," said Mr. Matthews. "I'll learn the last sentence by heart—it'll make a ripping excuse next time I do a dam' silly thing."

Cheques were drawn for Quillian and Pusely-Smythe, and the chairman then opened the envelope containing the problem that Leonard had set for the following month. It was entitled "The Handkerchief Problem," and on the face of it scarcely supported the theory that the ingenious Leonard was a Great Moral Teacher. The Hon. James Feldane was reminded that it would be his duty to preside on the next occasion and to adjudicate on this problem, which was as follows: "It is required to steal as many handkerchiefs as possible from a member or members of the Problem Club. Violence may not be used and thefts detected in the act will not score. Restitution will be made of the stolen handkerchiefs within twenty-four hours of the adjudication, but felonious intent is to be presumed in every case."

"Rotten luck," said Feldane, to his friend, Hesseltine. "I should have enjoyed working on this problem. It appeals to my natural instincts. I should probably have won it, and in that case might have given one or two of them something on account. And so this has to be the occasion when I'm shut out of the competition and have to act as chairman."

"Yes," said Hesseltine. "Nobody's so sure of himself as the non-starter."

No. V
The Handkerchief Problem

At the forty-seventh meeting of the Problem Club, the chair was taken by the youngest member, the Hon. James Feldane. That weary young gentleman having provided himself with a double portion of green Chartreuse, for the purpose, as he said, of supporting the dignity of the position, opened his adjudication a little informally.

"Let's get started," he said. "The first job is to read out the particular teaser with which the wily Leonard has been worrying you poor old things during the past month. Here goes."

The terms of the Handkerchief Problem were then read out. They were as follows: "It is required to steal as many handkerchiefs as possible from a member or members of the Problem Club. Violence may not be used and thefts detected in the act will not score. Restitution will be made of the stolen handkerchiefs within twenty-four hours of the adjudication, but felonious intent is to be presumed in every case."

"I wish I could have been a competitor this time," the chairman continued, "instead of being stuck up here to give the momentous decision. I should have had some sport, and handkerchief-sneaking falls nicely within my line of intellect; I might have scooped the prize. But as I'm debarred from scoring off you, I've taken jolly good care that none of you should score off me. For the past month every handkerchief I've used has been attached to the interior of the pocket by a steel chain and swivel, and those not in use have been locked away in a safe. My valet thinks I've gone off my head, of course, but then he'd have been bound to have thought that sooner or later, anyhow. The great point is that not one of you low pickpockets has been able to get a handkerchief out of me. We'll now pursue the inquiry. Hesseltine, are you guilty or not guilty?"

"Guilty, m'lord," said young Hesseltine cheerfully. "I may not be winner, but I think it would be safe to back me for a place. I struck early. At our last meeting, as soon as this problem was announced, I slipped stealthily and unobserved from the room. I had rightly concluded that there would be no attendant in the cloakroom at that hour. If there had been I should have sent him away to get me a box of matches. From the overcoats of members I secured a nice little haul of nine handkerchiefs. One of them, a silk bandanna, the property of Major Byles, was big enough for two, and ought to count as two."

"Might count two on a division, as they say at the elections," said the chairman. "But in the undivided state it counts one. Anything further to say?"

"That was my only coup. The only thing to add is that one of the nine belonged to a gentleman who did not start keeping them in the safe quite soon enough."

"All right," said Jimmy. "Speaking entirely *sotto voce* and *ex officio*, I'll be even with you for that one of these days. Meanwhile, Mr. Matthews, it will be your painful duty as secretary to give that thief a score of nine."

The chairman then called upon Mr. Quillian, K.C., whose story was connected with the story of Mr. Pusely-Smythe. In both cases it was a story of failure. Both men had hit on precisely the same idea.

Quillian called on Pusely-Smythe at a time when he knew he would be out, but would be expected back shortly. He, as he anticipated, was recognised by the servant and asked if he would wait. During the period of waiting Quillian made a swift and silent excursion to Pusely-Smythe's bedroom with a view to abstracting his available store of handkerchiefs. But the chairman was not the only member who had taken the precaution of keeping his handkerchiefs in an unlikely place. Not one solitary handkerchief could Quillian find. And while he was thus engaged Pusely-Smythe had been calling on Quillian with similar intentions, similar practice, and a similar result.

"You're both too clever to live," observed the chairman, "but you've cancelled one another for once. Mr. Harding Pope, as a politician, you should be familiar with the paths of dishonesty. How did you get on?"

The Member of Parliament gave a somewhat sickly smile.

"I fear," he said, "that I have not competed. I represent a Dissenting constituency, which is careful—almost to the point of being inquisitorial—as to my character and private life. Had I competed, it is easily possible that I might have been arrested. I could have explained, but all explanations come too late. It would have done me great injury. In the circumstances I have decided to resign my membership of this club, and my resignation will be in the chairman's hands at the next meeting. I have enjoyed these meetings immensely, but I have been—and am likely to be—too often debarred from taking an active part in the competition as a member should. The delightful but unscrupulous Leonard asks too much of me. Should I ever find myself in a position of greater freedom and less responsibility, I shall certainly crave the honour of re-election."

"Sorry," said the chairman. "I'm sure we all are. But the rules of the club do require that members shall be workers and not merely onlookers. If ever the political cat jumps the other way, and you're thrown out of Westminster into the cold, cold night, I make no doubt that at the first vacancy we shall welcome the lost sheep back to the nest. I will now call upon Major Byles."

The Major lived in the country. There were unusually good golf links in the neighbourhood, and he was both a good player and a good host. He had used his opportunities as he explained.

"I worked on a system. I waited till my man was absolutely wrapped up in the game, meanwhile locating his handkerchief carefully. Then, at the moment when he was following the ball with the eye, I put in some swift finger-work. It was not always successful. The Doctor, for instance, bowled me out twice—he's got eyes in the back of his head. But I got six handkerchiefs that way, and a seventh from a rain-coat that had been left in my hall. I've good reason to know that I'm not a winner, but it's not bad—eh?"

"A good sporting game," said the chairman. "These thefts from the person ought really to count more than easy overcoat-shots. They want more dexterity. The others only require brain-work. Still, I have to administer the law as Leonard lays it down. So far Hesseltine wins."

"But he won't win," said the Major mysteriously. "Oh, yes, I've got good reason to know it." And he proceeded to compound for himself a due measure of whisky and seltzer-water.

Dr. Alden, who was next called upon, could claim a score of only two. But so far as it went, it was brilliant and audacious work. One of the handkerchiefs had been taken from Sir Charles Bunford and one from Mr. Matthews, and in both cases the theft had been committed in Piccadilly in broad daylight and under the eyes of the police.

"It's clear where your real talent lies," said Jimmy. "You're wasted in Harley Street. However, time's getting on, and a few bad men would like a rubber of bridge before we part. Will any member who claims to have beaten Hesseltine's score kindly hold up a hand?"

The Rev. Septimus Cunliffe and Mr. Wildersley, A.R.A., both held up hands.

"What?" said the chairman. "Our padre in the sneak-thief business? Has he no respect for his cloth? Leonard has a lot to answer for. However, we will hear you, Mr. Cunliffe."

"Leonard," said that broad-minded cleric in his sonorous voice, "has once more revealed himself as a great moralist. He has shown us that the thief, a bad man, must none the less have good qualities, and has taught us to differentiate the good from the bad. The spirit of adventure, the clever planning, the manual dexterity displayed by the thief, are all worthy of praise. It is solely to his felonious intentions that we should take exception. Leonard has expressly provided that for the purposes of this competition the felonious intentions are to be purely imaginary; they are to be supposed. Consequently, I could approach the problem with a clear conscience. And I admit that in compiling a score of fourteen my cloth has been of assistance. Suspicion does not attach readily to a man in clerical attire.

"To proceed to my story, one Saturday, early in the month, I had been down to play golf with our friend, the Major. (By the way, you'll send me back my handkerchief, Major. Already in the post? Thanks.) On leaving his house I noticed at the back entrance a laundry van, in charge of a sleepy-looking rustic. The name and address of the laundry were proclaimed on the van in large letters. My knowledge of the country showed me that in approaching the Major's house that van would pass an inn called the Royal George, at a distance of two miles from the house, and a turning to the railway-station at a distance of one mile. That made everything easy. On the following Saturday I was on that road three miles from the house. My boots were dusty and I looked as tired as I could. I waited till the van came along, hailed it, and asked the driver to give me a lift as far as the station turning. He was not averse to making an extra shilling, and I climbed up. For the first mile I was talking to the man and making friends with him. When we reached The Royal George I suggested that a pint at my expense would not come amiss to him, and that I would look after the horse while he was inside. He was good enough to say that I was a parson after his own heart, and handed me the reins. The horse did not need any looking after; it was not that kind of horse. In the interior of the van I explored a laundry basket, and annexed fourteen of the Major's handkerchiefs. (I have left them in the cloak-room for you, Major.) When the driver came out I was holding the reins and looking pensive. I stepped off at the station turning. What is your decision, Mr. Chairman?"

"Brainy piece of work, and a fair score of fourteen. My idea was that nobody would get beyond fifteen. Did you beat that, Wildersley?"

That large but child-like artist smiled. "I claim a score of one hundred and forty-four."

"Gee-whizz! I didn't know there were so many handkerchiefs in the world. Which members did you get them from?"

"I got the whole lot from you, in spite of the steel chain and the locked safe."

"But I've not got as many. It's an impossibility. However, let's have the yarn."

"You'll find it's all right, Mr. Chairman. You young men are so careless that you don't know what you've got. Some time ago I had to execute a Deed of Gift—making over a rotten-cotton picture of mine to a provincial gallery. Up to that time I didn't know the difference between a Deed of Gift and a hole in a wall, but you learn things as you go on living. When this problem was set, I saw that by a Deed of Gift and a small investment I could do myself good. My first step was to buy twelve dozen handkerchiefs—top quality and deucedly expensive. I had a monogram of the chairman's initials excellently designed by myself and embroidered by the shop on all those handkerchiefs. This having been done, I collected my parcel of lingerie and went off to my solicitor, who is of the old-established, eighteen-carat type. I told him what I wanted, and the shock nearly killed him. When he got better I explained that it was a joke, but that it was essential in order to get the laugh that the Deed of Gift making over the handkerchiefs should be all correct, water-tight, and copper-bottomed. He does not understand jokes and will believe anything about them. So he engineered me a lovely Deed. I then addressed the parcel to the Hon. James Feldane, and went off with it in a taxi to Jimmy's place. I deposited the parcel, with the address downwards, on a chair in the hall, and put my overcoat and hat on the top of it. I then went in and had a few words with Jimmy about a bridge-problem. I had now made the handkerchiefs Jimmy's property by Deed of Gift. I had delivered them at his residence. It only remained to steal them, and that was easy. It's always easier to steal a thing if the owner doesn't know he's got it. Besides, as it was half-past eleven in the morning, Jimmy's costume consisted of a bath-gown, a Turkish cigarette, and a bad headache, which excused him from coming out into the hall with me when I left. I picked up my hat and coat, and a parcel containing one hundred and forty-four handkerchiefs, the property of the chairman, and went off. He will find the parcel returned to him when he gets home to-night. And I should like his decision."

"Much obliged to you, Wildersley. It's ironical that I can make a bit, as long as I'm not competing. All the same, the decision must be held up a moment. The fact that you've provided me with more handkerchiefs than I shall ever use this side of the silent tomb might influence my judicial mind. I must have a second opinion—counsel's. Will Mr. Quillian kindly give us his views on this claim."

"I don't usually give opinions in this offhand way," said Mr. Quillian, "but on this occasion I have really no doubt. The Deed, sir, was duly executed, so we are informed. The goods in question were *bona-fide* intended to become your property, and have in fact become so. They were delivered at your residence. In the absence of felonious intent I should say that they had not been stolen, but the terms of the problem state that felonious intent is to be presumed. Your ignorance of the whole transaction does not seem to me to affect it. In your place, sir, I should have no hesitation in finding the claim good—and I only wish I had thought of the idea myself—I ought to have done."

"Thank you, Mr. Quillian. Then I decide that Wildersley is the winner. Mr. Matthews, will you please draw the usual cheque to Mr. Wildersley's order?"

This having been done, and the chairman for the next meeting appointed, Jimmy opened the sealed envelope containing the problem that Leonard, the astute head-waiter, had set for the ensuing month.

Jimmy read it to himself first. "Well," he said, "this is a new line of country. This is somewhat of a sensation. It's called the Identity Problem, and runs as follows: 'It is required to discover the identity of Leonard. The use of professional detectives, and any communication with Leonard himself on the subject of this problem, are forbidden.'"

"I always knew," said Hesseltine, with conviction, "that chap was no ordinary headwaiter."

And it appeared that several other members, who also had forgotten to mention it before, had always been of the same opinion.

No. VI
The Identity Problem

The Rev. Septimus Cunliffe took the chair at the forty-eighth meeting of the Problem Club. The problem which Leonard, the astute head-waiter, had set the members to solve during the preceding month was simply the discovery of his own identity; and competitors were debarred from communicating with Leonard himself or from employing detectives in its solution.

Mr. Cunliffe, with a pardonable enjoyment of his own excellent elocution, read out the terms of the problem in tones that almost made it a drama. And the few introductory remarks that usually fell from the chairman became in his case almost an address. True, the occasion furnished him with some excuse.

"Gentlemen," he said, "with this meeting the Problem Club brings to a close the fourth year of its existence. The idea of the club, as I dare say most of you are aware, originated in the imaginative brain of Lord Herngill, and of the original members there are still three left us—Sir Charles Bunford, Major Byles, and Mr. Matthews. The eccentric nobleman who was our founder did not himself long remain a member. Broken in health and, as I understand, suffering from private disappointments, he relinquished his clubs and retired altogether from society. He spent the remainder of his days on his Yorkshire estate, shut out from the world and even denying himself the companionship of old friends. It was only a few months ago that his death was announced in the newspapers. A somewhat gloomy subject, gentlemen, but it seemed to me fitting that on this occasion we should recall with gratitude the name of our founder.

"Now for the first two years of the club's existence the monthly problem was always provided by the member whose duty it would be to adjudicate on it. But during the second year it was found that this did not work well. Some of the members had not sufficient readiness of invention. Others did not show sufficient discretion. Our minutes of that period show some problems, I grieve to say, that can only be described as scandalous. Under these circumstances a member, Mr. Barstairs, since dead, was deputed to find for us some able and trustworthy person who, for a small honorarium, would act as our setter of problems. At the next meeting he announced that he had selected Leonard, who had then just become head-waiter here.

"The selection of a head-waiter for the purpose seemed to some of us—certainly to myself—fantastic, more especially as Barstairs offered no explanation at all. But, we must admit, fantasy plays some part in the spirit of the club, and no formal objection was raised. Time has shown that Barstairs had reason in his fantasy. Leonard has given us every satisfaction. Whoever he may be, I think that we are agreed on one point—that he possesses qualities unusual in a headwaiter.

"In fact, gentlemen, the news that I am about to give you will, I am sure, be received with regret. I have a letter from Leonard in which he tells me that after eleven to-night he will cease to be in the service of the hotel, and will no longer be available as our problem-setter. He offers, if it would be any convenience to us, to name a successor whose ability and discretion he can guarantee absolutely. I may add that it is a very properly-expressed and respectful letter.

"The appointment of a successor may, I think, be considered later. Let us now proceed to the adjudication of the current competition. I confess that if I personally had to find out who Leonard is, I should not, under the conditions imposed, know how to begin. However, I have great confidence in the ingenuity of the ten members before me—there would have been eleven but for Harding Pope's resignation."

The chairman's confidence was misplaced. Every member had made an attempt to solve the problem, but every one had failed. Several of them had hit on the expedient of following Leonard when he left the hotel. The Hon. James Feldane, for example, had hit on it, and recounted his failure.

"I lay up in a taxi a few yards from the door of this place, where I could get a good view. Presently out came Leonard, and I might very easily have missed him, for I was expecting him to bob up from the basement, and he came out of the main entrance. He was well turned out, and looked rather less like a head-waiter than I do myself. He called up a taxi and got in. Off he went, and off I went after him, my driver having been instructed. We drove, as near as I can guess, for about umpty-ump hours. I know I began to wonder if my cigarettes would last out the trip. Then my cab slowed down to a crawl, and I looked cautiously from the window. Leonard's cab had stopped in front of a mouldy-looking place with big gilt letters on it. He overpaid his cabman—I heard the words, 'Thank you,' distinctly—ran up the steps, rang a bell, and entered. I got out.

"'Cabby,' I said, 'where are we? Is this the hereafter?'

"'No, sir,' he said. 'Looks like it, but it's really Brixton.'

"The big gilt letters informed me that Leonard had entered the Beaulieu Temperance Hotel. I pushed the push, and the door was half opened to me by an Italian waiter with the darkest eyes and hands I ever saw. I could catch a glimpse of a small hall furnished with a good deal of dust and a stand for hats and coats. I spotted Leonard's excellent hat and overcoat thereon. The waiter looked at me suspiciously. I got right on to the point at once.

"'I want,' I said, 'the name and address of the gentleman who came in here just now, and I'll pay a sovereign for it.'

"He seemed to understand the argument. In a minute he was back with the name and address and the information that the gentleman was stopping there for only one night. He got his sovereign. The name he gave was Leonard, and the address was the address of this hotel. I may have been more annoyed in the course of my life, but I doubt it. So I made the weary journey back again, had a light supper of one whisky and soda, and went to bed."

Mr. Matthews had followed Leonard on foot to the Ritz. Mr. Quillian had tracked him to a desperate hostelry in the far north of London. Major Byles had pursued him to an hotel in Wimbledon. They ascertained that he spent a night at each one of these three places, but they added nothing else to their knowledge of him.

Sir Charles Bunford had been no more successful, but he had a curious story to tell. He had met Leonard by chance in St James's Street one night at half-past eleven. There was nothing in Leonard's dress or bearing that suggested anything less than complete independence. Sir Charles felt certain that he himself had not been recognised, turned, and followed him.

"He led me," Sir Charles recounted, "up through the squares to Oxford Street, where he turned west. Just then there came shuffling along in the gutter towards us a street-vendor with a tray of little toys slung from his shoulders. He gave me the impression of an old man. Leonard and he both stopped. I also stopped, making a pretence of lighting a cigarette. They were both in the full light of a street lamp, and I had a close view of them. Leonard picked up from the tray a little monkey of blue plush mounted on a pin. Deliberately and without a smile he stuck the monkey in the gutter-merchant's battered bowler. Then he took out his notecase, produced a fiver, and spread it on the tray, and walked on. During this curious incident neither of the men spoke. As you may imagine, I tackled the street-vendor at once.

"'You're in luck,' I said. 'Did you know that customer?'

"He folded his fiver and slipped it into an inner pocket. He looked at me shrewdly, and I noticed that his eyes were young. His voice when he spoke was quite young. And it was the voice of an educated man too.

"'Which of us,' he said, 'can say that he knows the other—or even that he knows himself?'

"'Come,' I said. 'I think you can tell me what I want to know. And two fivers are better than one.'

"'That is so—to some people at some times—but not to Mr. William Bunting, the editor of *The Pig-Keepers' Friend*, at this time. I will wish you good-night, Sir Charles.'

"And he walked off briskly without a trace of the old slouch. How he knew my name I can't tell you, for certainly Leonard, even if he knew I was following, never said a word to him. The man left me staggered. I rushed off again after Leonard, but I had lost him. That is all I have to tell, and I have given you the facts accurately as they happened. I was both sane and sober at the time—but if you doubt that, upon my word I can't be surprised."

The failure was general. Dr. Alden had interviewed the proprietor of the hotel, who was most courteous, but, in the doctor's opinion, lied in his profession of ignorance. Mr. Pusely-Smythe got hold of one of the other waiters who appeared perfectly willing to betray anybody on the most moderate terms, but, unfortunately, had no information to impart.

"Well," said the chairman, "I must decide that the problem has not been solved. The prize for it not being awarded, the prize for the next competition is doubled. We have now to obtain the solution of the problem from the wily Leonard himself, and at the same time he is required to show us that the problem was possible of solution by us. It is now twenty to eleven and presumably Leonard leaves this hotel at eleven; so we have not much time to spare. If you, Mr. Quillian, will unlock the doors and ring the bell, I will tell the waiter that we should be glad to see Leonard for a few minutes."

But it was Leonard himself who answered the bell. He was a tall young man of good figure. He had not the stereotyped version of good looks, but his face was pleasing and full of humour and intelligence. He carried himself well. His dress was unsuited to the occasion, for he wore a well-cut lounge-suit of dark-blue cloth, and his brown, laced boots suggested a product of Bond Street intended for use in the country. There was no trace of a waiter about him. His manner was easy, confident without being assuming, and marked just by that touch of restraint that a man might show on first introduction to a number of his equals.

"Well, Leonard," said the chairman, "we were on the point of sending for you. Your problem has beaten us. Can you show us how we might have solved it, and provide us with the solution?"

"Certainly," said Leonard. "I'd rather expected that I should be wanted."

"Good. Now sit down, won't you? We're all quite informal here."

"Thanks," said Leonard. It seemed to be tacitly and generally accepted that he had become a guest of the club. Dr. Alden proffered his cigar-case; Jimmy brought him a whisky-and-soda.

"I think I ought to begin," said Leonard, "by apologising to you for having given you all such a lot of trouble—more especially as it was quite intentional on my part."

"Part of the game," said Major Byles. "That's all right. No apologies needed."

"Thanks very much. At any rate I can apologise for these clothes. The fact is that I'm going North by the midnight train from Euston, and so I changed. And now let me show one or two ways in which the problem could have been solved. Some of you followed me when I took a taxi to an outlying hotel, and subsequently made applications at the hotel. If, instead of doing this, you had hailed the taxi that I had just left, you would in each case have found inside it an addressed envelope giving you the information you required. When Mr. Feldane went for that very long drive to Brixton, I intentionally left my hat and coat in the hall of the alleged hotel for a few minutes. He examined the waiter; if he had examined the inside of my hat he would have found a certain clue. Sir Charles very nearly caught me. That night I left the hotel much earlier than usual, and had satisfied myself that nobody was waiting for me outside. I was on my way to a house in Audley Street where I was not known as the head-waiter at this hotel, and my identity would probably have been discovered; and it was necessary I should go to that house. At the top of St. James's Street I found that Sir Charles was after me. But I had taken a precaution. A friend of mine was stationed in Oxford Street, masquerading as a vender of penny plush monkeys; I found him and we went through a little eccentric pantomime together that had been prearranged. As had

been expected, Sir Charles stopped to make inquiries from him.
And while that was happening I made my escape."

"One moment," said Sir Charles. "How on earth did he know
who I was? You never spoke to him?"

"No, I never spoke. And he did not know who you were. He did
not know that you were Sir Charles Bunford, and does not know it
now. He knew that he could address you as Sir Charles, and he
knew that from the fact that I stuck the monkey in his hat. It was a
prearranged code. If Major Byles had been following me, I should
have stuck the monkey in my friend's right sleeve. He would then
have addressed him as Major, though he would not have known
his name. If Mr. Wildersley had been after me, the monkey would
have gone into the left sleeve; my friend would have known by that
sign that he was an artist, but would have known no more than
that. Similarly, in other cases, he would always have appeared to
have known, but would not have known really."

"Leonard," said the chairman, "in my opinion you have shown
both skill and discretion, and a good sporting spirit besides. I
decide that your problem was fair. And now will you solve it for
us?"

"Very good. I must give you some abbreviated family history.
My grandfather had two sons, both of whom disappointed him,
though in different ways. My uncle was a man of extreme avarice;
my father, the younger of the two, was a gambler. Both my parents
died before I was five years old, and I—the only child—passed into
the charge of my grandfather.

"My grandfather placed me with the family of an intimate friend
of his, who was also the senior partner in the firm of solicitors who
acted for him, a Mr. Barstairs. Barstairs had married a French-
woman. French was the language generally spoken in their house,
and most of my early years were spent abroad. I went through a
public-school and Cambridge without any particular disgrace or
distinction. So far, my grandfather had kept me well supplied with
money; in fact, at Cambridge I had not spent my allowance. But I
had never seen my grandfather. I wrote to him four times a year,

and his replies were always witty and entertaining. I took everything for granted in the way that boys do.

"On my twenty-first birthday I had a letter from my grandfather to the effect that as an experiment he wished me to make my own living in any way I liked for a period of some years. When that period was over, or sooner if he died before then, I was to be no longer under that necessity. Mr. Barstairs, who had not been consulted, was indignant about that letter, but I did not resent it myself.

"What assets had I to offer an employer? My classical degree would have entitled me to teach in a school—a truly awful profession to my mind. I spoke two Continental languages well and a third passably. I had an unusual knowledge of wines and cuisine for a man of my age. (Mr. Matthews will remember that Barstairs was an epicure.) I had seen a good deal of hotel life at home and abroad. I took counsel with Mr. Hance, the proprietor of this hotel, who was known to me. After some training at an hotel in Paris I became the night head-waiter here, using my first name, Leonard, as my surname. My grandfather and Mr. Barstairs alone were taken into my secret. It is to the latter that I owe the pleasure of having served a club of which I should be proud one day to become a member, if that were possible. I saw life from a novel and interesting angle. I had my mornings free for poetry, to which I am devoted. I was quite satisfied.

"There is little more to add. In the year that I came here my uncle died unmarried. Three months ago my grandfather also died, and I—"

"Pardon me," said Sir Charles, "but I have been watching your face carefully, and I think I see a family likeness or the trace of one. All that you have said would confirm it. I think you are the grandson of the founder of this club, and in that case you are the sixth Baron Herngill."

"That is correct. I remained here for these months while some legal matters were completed, and to oblige Hance, for I consider that he did me a good turn. I leave for Enthwaite to-night. And now, gentlemen, since time presses, may I mention that I have a successor to myself to propose to you, if you have made no other arrangements? He would act on the same terms as I have done. I will answer for his ability and discretion. He is, like myself, a poet. He is also the editor of an obscure weekly publication called *The Pig-Keepers' Friend*. If you choose him I have here his first problem to deliver to the chairman. His name is William Bunting. With your permission I will retire for a few minutes while you consider this."

When he had gone out it was found that every member of the Problem Club had formed the same idea. On his return to the room Lord Herngill was informed that Mr. Bunting had been appointed, and also that Lord Herngill had been proposed by the chairman, seconded by Sir Charles Bunford, and unanimously elected a member of the Problem Club.

No. VII
The Shakespearean Problem

The failure of the members to discover the identity of Leonard—the last problem that he had set them—meant that at the forty-ninth meeting the prize was doubled, and a cheque for two hundred and twenty pounds awaited the lucky winner. Leonard, formerly known as a capable head-waiter and an astute setter of problems, had revealed himself as the grandson and heir of the Lord Herngill who had founded the club, and had been elected to membership. He had described himself further as a poet. He had now traveled up from Yorkshire for the express purpose of attending the first meeting after his election, and the dinner with which the proceedings opened showed him, as had been expected, a charming, accomplished, and quite amusing companion.

Young Hesseltine and the Rev. Septimus Cunliffe were, respectively, chairman and secretary for the evening. The chairman, equipped with a bound copy of Shakespeare, and certain other forms of refreshment, read out the terms of the competition. They were longer than usual, and ran as follows:—

"Members are required, in the course of conversation, to make undetected quotations from Shakespeare, and to detect and challenge the quotations which are made by other members.

"The score is two for making an undetected quotation, and one for detecting and challenging a quotation made by another. The highest score wins. If any member challenges as a quotation from Shakespeare words which are not a quotation from that author, he will have one deducted from his score. Any member with a score of minus three is out of the game.

"The method of challenging will be by raising one hand, when the chairman will temporarily arrest proceedings and investigate. Where several members raise their hands simultaneously, all will score the detection, or be penalised for the failure, as the case may be. Otherwise, only the first hand up can score or be penalised.

"A quotation must consist of more than four words, or it will not rank as a quotation. The words must be given in their correct order, but otherwise any attempt may be made to disguise the quotation. Any member who has made an undetected quotation should notify it to the chairman at the earliest opportunity, while it is still fresh in the memory.

"Detection, to be valid, should be made immediately—say, within twenty seconds of the utterance of the quotation.

"The chairman will stop the competition when in his opinion all members have had a fair and full chance of speaking, and on all disputed points his ruling is absolute."

"Yes," said the chairman, when he had read out the above, "our new problem-setter, the mysterious editor of *The Pig-Keepers' Friend*, seems to be rather a lengthy beggar. More like a round game than a problem, to my mind. I can imagine literary circles playing it on winter evenings. However, I think we've most of us got the hang of it. There's double the usual amount of boodle in the jack-pot, but all the same I'm not sorry to be debarred from competing. I had a good deal of Shakespeare boosted into me by schoolmasters when I was a boy, but I fear that it ain't stuck to me. Well, it's all up to the high-brows to-night. And I'll call on our old friend Leonard, who's our new member, Lord Herngill, to start the ball rolling, and our padre to keep the score as directed."

"Well," said Leonard, "I can't say that I am a stranger here, but I am certainly a new member, and very glad to be. Now, I told you that I was a poet, but a writer of poetry is not necessarily a reader of poetry. I can't say whether he ought to be or not." He paused to relight a cigarette. "To be candid—"

"I challenge," said Mr. Cunliffe, with uplifted hand. "The quotation is, 'To be or not to be,' rather cunningly broken up."

"Admitted," said Leonard.

"Then," said the chairman, "the secretary will score one to himself."

"At the same time," said Leonard, "I should like him to score two to me. The words, 'I am a stranger here,' are a quotation from King Richard II, Act 2, Scene iii. Northumberland speaks them. And the quotation was not recognised."

This was verified and found correct and the score allowed. The chairman turned to the Hon. James Feldane, who was sitting—or, to be accurate, reclining—in the chair next to Leonard. "Go ahead, Jimmy," he said.

"Very well," said Jimmy wearily. "The—er—the quality of mercy—"

Five hands went into the air together.

"Jimmy," said the chairman, "it looks as if you were pretty considerably challenged—by five simultaneously. You, Major Byles, being one of them, will tell us why."

"Why?" exclaimed the Major. "Because it's one of the best-known quotations in Shakespeare. I won't swear which play it comes from, but everybody knows it. Let's see, how does it go? 'The quality of mercy is not strained, but droppeth like the thingamy of the something-or-other.'"

"Any defence, Jimmy?" asked the chairman.

"Somewhat," said Jimmy. "I said, 'The quality of mercy.' I admit it. I glory in it. But that's only four words, and it's laid down that four words do not make a quotation."

"That is so. I fear that the Major, Dr. Alden, our only K.C., and our two artist-members must all have a minus one recorded against them."

"What I was going to have said when they interrupted me was that the quality of mercy differed in some material respects from coffee that has been made with a percolator. Same thought as Shakey's, but a different mode of expression. Five of you have now lost a life through being premature. You need to be careful. A score of minus three puts you outside of any chance of two hundred and twenty of the very best. And I'm dangerous to-night—I'm out for blood. The brindled cat winds slowly o'er the lea—anybody like to challenge that?"

Wildersley said it would make a good title for an Academy picture, but nobody asserted that it was Shakespeare—not even Jimmy.

"You're an unenterprising lot," said Jimmy disdainfully. "But I'll give you one more chance.. 'Satiate at length, and heightened as with wine.' That's more than four words. Any challengers?"

"Yes," said Sir Charles, holding up his hand. "I don't know for certain, but it's got the flavour of the period in it. Anyway, I'd sooner lose one life than let you score a triumphant two for it."

"Then you'll lose the life. It's a quotation all right, but it happens to be a little bit that I cut out of the best end of *Paradise Lost,* by J. Milton, Esquire." And Jimmy leant back in his chair satisfied. He had scored nothing for himself, but he had done something to spoil the chances of six other men.

The chairman turned to Sir Charles. "Don't you think that Jimmy's an irreverent young blackguard?" he asked.

"Well," said Sir Charles, with an air of quiet dignity. "Jimmy is young and I am old. As we progress on life's journey, we old men cease to expect to find universal agreement with our views. We know that our opinions are our own, but cannot be all the world's." He paused and sighed. "A stage or two farther on, and Jimmy may come to think, as I do now, that—"

And here suddenly Sir Charles broke off and chuckled. "Well, I'm blest!" he said. "I never expected to do it. I knew this wasn't a little nest of Shakespeareans, but I did think that you'd spot the best-known line in Shakespeare."

That air of pathetic dignity had merely been a bit of acting, but the acting had been so good that it had distracted the attention from the words. Otherwise members must have found in Sir Charles's remarks the well-worn tag that "All the world's a stage." It scored two for Sir Charles, thus putting him on the way to a win, at any rate.

A few minutes later another well-known quotation very nearly came through unscathed. Somebody, speaking of Leonard, had said, "Leonard, or Lord Herngill, whichever he prefers to be called."

Leonard smilingly said that a rose by any other name would smell as sweet. He admitted afterwards that he had not had the slightest intention of quoting Shakespeare. He had merely uttered a platitude because it happened to be apt, though as soon as he said it he recognised his own quotation. Unfortunately for him, the Rev. Septimus Cunliffe had also recognised it, and by challenging it added one to a score that was growing slowly but surely. He attempted no quotation himself, and never challenged unless he was sure. To put it plainly, he played for safety.

"Yes," said Jimmy Feldane plaintively, commenting on this incident, "one of the worst points about Mr. W. Shakespeare is that he made such a lot of proverbs. I don't want to brag, but I suppose I've read as little as most people, and I expect that even I don't keep clear of Shakespearean quotations altogether. I'm not aiming at him, but every now and then he flies into it, so to speak."

The supercilious Mr. Quillian had provided himself with a stock of quotations from Elizabethan dramatists other than Shakespeare, and did deadly work with them. They were challenged, and brought the penalty on the challengers. And having thus inspired a dread of traps, he introduced three quotations which really were from Shakespeare, and two of them got through undetected. Pusely-Smythe, who generally welcomed a chance of a friendly duel with Quillian, remained silent, watching him with sardonic amusement.

The game became very strenuous. There was the closest attention in order to spot any veritable quotation. Every strategic dodge that had been thought of during the previous month was brought into action, to induce a challenge that would be penalised, or to get a quotation through undetected. Several members reached minus three, and were ruled out.

"This game is too much for me," said Mr. Matthews, on losing his third life. "It's too subtle. The American game of draw-poker, with three jokers in the pack and one of the players a crook, is simple, transparent, and childlike compared to it. However, one of the joys of being out of it is that I can get myself that little drink that I have long needed." And he made his way to the side-table.

"Mr. Chairman," said Sir Charles, "I think a ten-minutes' interval would be welcome. It's wearing work to keep on thinking what one is saying."

His suggestion was warmly supported and accepted by the chairman. Some members followed the comfortable example of Mr. Matthews. Some chuckled over the clever caricatures, drawn on the back of bridge-markers, with which Wildersley had been occupying his enforced leisure; an excess of zeal over discretion had put him out of the game at an early stage. All consulted the secretary's score-sheet. Quillian was leading with a score of nine. The secretary and Sir Charles were each at eight. Major Byles was three, and Pusely-Smythe one. Jimmy Feldane was minus one, and Lord Herngill—who had at one time reached the noble score of four—had by reckless challenging brought himself to the perilous position of minus two.

"Can't make it out," said Mr. Matthews to him. "You used to set all our problems. You ought to be a flyer at this kind of a game."

"It's an easy job to set problems," said Leonard, "and to set them so that you can solve them, but it's a different thing altogether to solve the problems that somebody else has set."

"Oh, well, it's an open thing still. Quillian's just leading, but I don't believe he'll pull it off. Shan't be surprised if old Bunford is two hundred and twenty the richer before the evening's out."

Proceedings were now resumed. "Come, now, Pusely-Smythe," said the chairman, "we've not heard much from you to-night."

"Afraid of being challenged?" suggested Quillian.

"As a rule," said Pusely-Smythe angrily, "I'm told that I am much too venturous. However, my learned friend, if you want to talk, go on and I will wait for you. The chairman called on me to speak, not you, and as a matter of fact, I had a thing to say. But let it go—it may make trouble later, and then you'll remember I told you what would come of this. Your blessed challenges, indeed! You may think you can do everything, but I know you can do very little."

Quillian stared at him aghast and perplexed.

"Really," he said, "I don't understand this outburst. I had not the slightest intention—"

But here he was interrupted by Pusely-Smythe's laughter. "All right, old man," said Pusely-Smythe cheerily. "Don't worry. It was all spoof and part of the game. Thanks to you, I've just made five undetected quotations from the work of the bard. You're my benefactor. In fact, as the Orientals say, you are my father and my mother, and I am the son of a dog."

"Five?" said the chairman. "It hardly seems possible."

But Pusely-Smythe made out his list and it was found to be quite correct. The five quotations were as follows:—

"I am much too venturous," *King Henry VIII.*, Act I, Scene ii.

"And I will wait for you," *Julius Caesar*, Act I, Scene ii.

"I had a thing to say—but let it go," *King John*, Act 3, Scene iii.

"I told you what would come of this," *The Winter's Tale*, Act 4, Scene iii.

"I know you can do very little," *Coriolanus*, Act 2, Scene i.

"It's a great *coup*," said the chairman. "It puts you right at the head of the list. Closing time is imminent, gentlemen. So if you have anything else to say, get on with it."

"Well," said Quillian, "somebody ought to have spotted him. It's really more our carelessness than his cleverness. But I should imagine that's the last undetected quotation he will be able to get through to-night. You're a watched man now."

"By Jove, yes," said the Major.

"Since you talk like that," said Pusely-Smythe, smiling. "I will make another quotation. By the way, how long will you give me? I should have asked you that before, of course."

"Five minutes," said the Major. "And then perhaps we might close the competition, if the chairman sees fit."

A general agreement was reached on this point, and Pusely-Smythe was enjoined by the chairman to get on with it. "I've finished, thanks," said Pusely-Smythe. "The words, 'I should have asked you that before,' are a quotation from a play called Romeo and Juliet. It's the second scene of the first act—Romeo speaking."

The quotation was verified, and advanced Pusely-Smythe's score to thirteen—a lucky number for once—thus leaving him an easy winner.

"And," said young Hesseltine, the chairman, as he handed him the cheque, "considering the way you must have sweated through tons and tons of absolute Shakespeare during the month, in order to pick out the little bits that didn't look like quotations, I'm not sure that you haven't earned about five per cent. of it."

The chairman now opened the sealed envelope containing the problem for the next month. In this the talented editor of *The Pig-Keepers' Friend* had been quite brief. It was entitled "The Impersonation Problem," and the terms of it were as follows:—

"It is required to be mistaken for six different people in the course of one hour."

"He don't use any unnecessary words about it," said Mr. Matthews.

But it may be remembered that the editor of *The Pig-Keepers' Friend* was also a poet—and real poets never use unnecessary words.

No. VIII
The Impersonation Problem

The terms of the Impersonation Problem, which came up for adjudication at the fiftieth meeting of the club, were as follows:—

"It is required to be mistaken for six different people in the course of one hour."

Mr. Wildersley, A.R.A.—large, cheerful, and childlike—took the chair, and observed that it was just as well for other members that the dignified position of adjudicator prevented him from competing, as otherwise he would have been a certain winner. It was a claim that the chairman for the evening very frequently made, but Wildersley was not very serious about it.

"My profession," he said, "would have given me a start of about eighty yards in the hundred. I'm skilled in the rapid use of oil paints. Within the prescribed limit of one hour I could have painted myself to look like a rabbit, or a tomato, or a man, or a hole in the ground, or any other object of the seashore, so as absolutely to defy detection. Not one of you duffers would have had a chance."

"Pardon the interruption," said Mr. Quillian, K.C., "but the terms of the problem require us to be mistaken for six different people. May I ask the chairman if he would consider a rabbit and a tomato as being people for the purposes of this problem?"

"The time of the chairman," said Wildersley, severely, "is not to be wasted on purely hypothetical cases. If, when his turn comes, Mr. Quillian claims to have been mistaken for a rabbit, I shall be ready both to believe it and to adjudicate upon it. And now, gentlemen, we will have the story of your dismal failures. Hesseltine here

103

is acting as secretary to-night, and he may as well get his talking done first, so that he can give his undivided attention to his duties."

"Well," said Hesseltine, "Feldane and I went into partnership this time, as the rules permit. We don't claim to have scored the full six, but we had a lovely time while it lasted. Jimmy had better tell you about it, as he played the lead."

"Yes," said Jimmy, with a weary smile, "it was quite on the amusing side. Involved a lot of work though—thinking it all out and getting together the properties for the drama. If we scooped fifty-five pounds each over it we shouldn't be overpaid, but just as we were doing nicely the bottom fell out of it. However, I'll tell you."

The incidents which Jimmy related were as follows: Early on a fine morning he and Hesseltine were conveyed by a taxi-cab to a point, previously selected, on a road on the outskirts of a south-western suburb. Here they unloaded their miscellaneous collection of properties and got to work. The driver took the cab off to a public-house in the vicinity, and there awaited further orders.

Hesseltine was disguised as a labourer. Jimmy, who was to act as his boss, was got up as, to use his own description, "a sort of semi-scientific clerky person, clad in a seedy suit, a pince-nez, and an air of educated wisdom." They began by enclosing a portion of the roadway with stakes and ropes, fixing red flags at the corners of the square. Then Hesseltine entered the enclosure and began vigorously to dig a hole in the road with pick and spade. It was still early, and there were few people about. So Hesseltine's boss condescended to lend a hand with the digging. Afterwards Feldane contented himself with strolling round the hole with a voltmeter, borrowed from the taxi-cab, in one hand, a two-foot rule sticking out of his breast-pocket, and a general air of importance.

When the hole was about three feet deep a sleepy policeman paused on his way past.

"Something wrong with the drains?" he asked.

"Hope not," said Feldane cheerfully. "But that's what we're going to find out. We're just putting in the smoke-test on this section."

"I see," said the policeman. "You ain't from Mackworth's, are you?"

"Mackworth's? Oh, no. We're from Matthews and Byles, the sanitary engineers at Vauxhall. Dare say you know the name."

The policeman said he believed he'd heard it, and passed on. The game had now definitely begun, and there was only one hour to play it in and no time to be lost. A small car was approaching with a lady driving. Feldane ran into the road, held up his hand, and stopped it.

"Sorry, madam," he said to the lady, "but would you mind waiting just for a few seconds? I'm sure you'll understand. We've got an Erichsen's galvanometrical balance working in that hole, and the least vibration would spoil the reading. We shan't be a minute."

"Certainly," said the lady. "I know something of these delicate instruments. What are you using it for?"

"We're from the Post Office Electrical Survey. There's trouble with the telegraph wires here that they can't locate. Of course if iron pyrites has been used in the construction of the road, that would account for it. We're looking into it. Bill," he called to Hesseltine, "what do you make it?"

Hesseltine examined the bottom of the hole. "Steady at two point five," he called back.

"Good. Let this car past, and then set a foot further in. Thank you very much, madam."

The unsuspecting lady drove on. Hesseltine sat down in the hole and laughed. Jimmy glanced at his watch. "That's two in under ten minutes," he said. "If we can keep it up at anything like this rate, we ought to do."

But for some time after this passers-by proved curious but unenterprising. They stared with the keenest interest at the proceedings, but did not put in any inquiry. Then an elderly tramp paused on his way into the town.

"Water-main?" he suggested.

"Ay," said Jimmy.

"All that work for a little water! Sooner you than me."

Almost immediately afterwards a rather fussy and important little man demanded to know what it was all about.

"Gas," said Jimmy laconically. "There's no gas-main in this road," snapped the little man.

"No," said Jimmy. "Nor likely to be until we've took the level for the pipes. Pass along, please."

The little man said that it seemed hopeless to expect a civil answer to a civil question nowadays, but he passed along. Jimmy again consulted his watch.

"Four in half an hour," he observed. "We can hardly miss it now."

But fate was already on its way in the shape of a young, newly-appointed, eager and suspicious policeman. He watched Jimmy and Hesseltine for a minute or so in silence. Jimmy made an entry in a pocket-book.

"All right, Bill," said Jimmy to Hesseltine. "You can fill in again now."

"What do you think you're doing?" asked the policeman.

"Rubberite Road Construction," said Jimmy. "They're putting down an experimental section here, and this is just the preliminary testing."

"Don't they put no notice-board up with the name of the firm on?"

"They will, of course, as soon as the actual work begins. I have their card." This printed card had been one of Jimmy's properties. The policeman slipped it into his pocket.

"I've no doubt it's all right," said the policeman, "but I'll just show this card to make sure."

"Certainly," said Jimmy; "that's the thing to do. You'll find they know all about it up at the station."

The game was up. As soon as the policeman was round the corner Jimmy dashed off to fetch the taxi while Hesseltine completed the work of filling in the hole and getting their various properties together. They had at least the satisfaction of getting clear away before the policeman returned.

The chairman, when he had heard the story, said that if everybody had their rights it was probable that two of the younger members of the Problem Club would now be in prison, but he would allow them a score of five all the same. The fifth score might seem a little doubtful, but the young policeman has said that he believed it was all right, and if he had not would probably have taken stronger measures. The chairman also refused to admit Quillian's objection that the conspirators had been mistaken for imaginary people. People might be real or imaginary, and the subtle editor of *The Pig-Keepers' Friend* had not indicated that either meaning was excluded. A further protest by Major Byles and Mr. Matthews against the scandalous use that had been made of their names for the firm of sanitary engineers was not taken seriously.

But the Major may have been embittered by the completeness of his own failure. With the help of a gray wig and beard and some shabby clothes, he had intended to call at six different back-doors and to represent in succession six different people—a beggar, a fortune-teller, a vendor of cheap jewelry, and so forth. But the first back-door at which he called was his own, and there he was immediately recognised by a house-dog and by his own kitchen-maid. His subsequent explanation that he had merely been doing it for a bet had not been well received. He did not give details, but it was gathered that Mrs. Byles had had a good deal to say on the subject.

Lord Herngill had done very little better. He had attempted no disguise at all. His idea had been, in the course of travel on the Bakerloo Tube railway, to get into conversation with six different people and to tell six plausible but erroneous stories about himself. His statement that he personally had driven the first train that had passed under the Thames in that tube, being in fact the consulting engineer of the company, was received by an old lady with great interest and not the slightest suspicion. He then changed into another carriage and found an opportunity to tell a young curate that though he lived within ten miles of London he had never been there in his life before. He was only there then because he had to see property that he had inherited at Swiss Cottage. And could the curate tell him at all where Swiss Cottage was?

That question was his undoing. "I can not only tell you," said the smiling curate, "but, as it happens, I am going there myself, and it will give me much pleasure to have your company."

And by the time that he had got rid of that curate it was hopeless to attempt his remaining impersonations within the prescribed time. It was generally felt that in a matter of impersonation Lord Herngill, on his previous character, should have done better.

Mr. Quillian had bestowed six shillings on six different crossing-sweepers. Five of them had said, "Thank you, m'lord," and the other had said, "Thank you, Captain." On this he claimed to have won, as it was obvious that all five crossing-sweepers could not have mistaken him for the same peer. It was pointed out to him by the chairman that there was not the slightest evidence that any one of those crossing-sweepers had made any mistake at all.

For once Pusely-Smythe had failed to compete, and said that he had been too busy. It was suggested that his time had been taken up with spending his winnings from the previous month. Mr. Matthews also had taken no part in the competition. The reason he gave was simple cowardice; the ghastly breakdown of his attempt to impersonate an old lady for the purposes of the Kiss Problem had spoiled his nerve for anything of the kind in the future.

The disgraceful adventure of Feldane and Hesseltine seemed likely to be the nearest approach to the problem-setter's requirements, until Sir Charles Bunford was called on for his experiences. Sir Charles claimed to have won.

"I came to the conclusion," said Sir Charles, "that the man who asks for something or tries to sell something is likely to create an atmosphere of suspicion. On the other hand the man who gives something, even to a complete stranger, will have his explanatory story accepted without question. The fact that he stands to lose by the transaction is accepted as evidence of his genuineness.

"With this conviction, and with such disguise as I thought advisable, I called at various houses all in one row in the Willesden neighbourhood. I was accompanied by a covered handcart, propelled by a boy hired for the purpose. Inside the handcart were the gifts that I had prepared for the occupants of the houses. Taking from the handcart a fruitcake in a paper bag, I rang at the first house and requested the dirty little girl who opened it to fetch her dear mamma. Mamma appeared, wiping her hands on her apron, and looking displeased with life in general and me in particular.

"'Good-morning, lady,' I said. 'I am instructed by my employers to ask you if you will do them the favour of accepting as a

THE PROBLEM CLUB 109

present this fruitcake of their manufacture. They are shortly open-
ing a branch in this neighbourhood and are taking this method of
making ladies acquainted with the quality of their goods. It is, in
fact, an advertisement.' After assuring herself again that there was
nothing to pay, and that the consumption of the cake would not
bind her to deal with my firm—Messrs. Butterstone and Co.—in
future, she consented to accept the cake, and even to say that it
seemed a straight way of doing business. She inquired where the
new shop would be, which I told her, and what the price of a similar cake would be if she ever wanted to buy one. I put it at half
what I had paid for it, and she said it was a pleasant morning. Never
for one moment did she doubt that I was what I had represented
myself to be.

"At the next house with equal success I presented half a pound
of butter as a sample of the products of the Farm Creameries Company, and a similar story. The third house got a tablet of scented
soap from an enterprising chemist who was just starting in business in the neighbourhood. At the next three houses I distributed
as free advertising samples a pound of sausages, a box of cigarettes,
and a small bottle of whisky. It took longer than I had expected,
because the ladies had such a lot of questions to ask about the new
shops that were to be opened, but I finished six minutes under the
hour. Of course, I could have carried all the goods round in a basket, but the handcart looked more like a house-to-house distribu-
tion on a large scale."

The decision was not given in his favour until after Quillian
had raised an objection. He maintained that in each case Sir
Charles had been mistaken for the same thing—to wit, the repre-
sentative or agent in advance of a business firm. But the chairman's
decision that Sir Charles had been mistaken for six different rep-
resentatives of six different firms was generally approved. And as no
other member had a claim to make the cheque was handed to him.

The chairman then opened the sealed envelope containing the
problem on which their ingenuity was next to be expended. It was
entitled "The Alibi Problem," and the terms of it were as follows:—

"It is impossible for a man to be in two places at once. But it is
required so to arrange matters that *bona-fide* evidence would be

procurable that at a certain hour of a certain day or night you were
in two places at once, the two places to be not less than one hundred miles from each other.”

“Not uninteresting,” said the Rev. Septimus Cunliffe, “but it
leaves a good deal to the discretion of the chairman. He will have
to decide which of us could produce the best evidence that the
impossible had been accomplished. By the way, who is the next
chairman?”

“Should have been Harding Pope,” said Wildersley. “But as he’s
gone, it will be the member elected in his place—our old friend
Leonard, Lord Herngill.”

“My poor abilities are at your service,” said Lord Herngill,
laughing, “at London’s lowest prices always.”

No. IX
The Alibi Problem

Lord Herngill read out the demand made by the editor of *The Pig-Keepers' Friend* on the ingenuity of the members of the Problem Club. Members were required to produce evidence, that could be given in good faith, that at a certain hour, day or night, they had been in two places at once, the two places not being less than one hundred miles apart.

Lord Herngill said that he felt anxious and depressed. His manner and appearance, it may be added, hardly bore out the statement. He assigned his depression to two reasons. Firstly, other chairmen had had the simple task of adjudicating on a point of fact. He—a new member, a novice, a mere babe, as you might say—was required to undertake far more delicate and difficult work, and to base his decision on an estimate of evidence. Secondly, the secretary for the evening was Mr. Wildersley. On the last occasion that Wildersley had acted as secretary he had adorned the minute-book with drawings of the chairman which were undoubtedly amusing and possessed of artistic merit, but at the same time were calculated to bring that chairman into ridicule and contempt.

"So you see, gentlemen," Lord Herngill continued, "that this is nervous work for me. However, I will make the plunge. Towards the end of dinner a telegram was handed to Mr. Feldane over which I noticed him to be chuckling. May I inquire if it had any bearing on the problem before us?"

"Well, it had," Jimmy admitted. "Brainy work to have guessed it. But I'm not on in this act—I'm resting. The wire really concerns Hesseltine's claim."

"You two generally hunt in couples. Perhaps Mr. Hesseltine will let you put his case for him."

"Anything that pleases you and saves me trouble," said Hesseltine generously. "I can always correct Jimmy if he makes an ass of himself."

"Well," said Jimmy, "we can see for ourselves that Hesseltine is here to-night. I don't want to dwell on his misfortunes, but he looks much as usual. Talks in the same silly way too. But that telegram is his evidence that he is really in Liverpool. It is signed with his name and was handed in at a Liverpool office. I'll read it. 'So sorry to be unable to be with you to-night, but have promised to remain here to act as judge at local baby-show.' Well, it isn't for me to say anything, though I could."

"The evidence that Mr. Hesseltine is here," said the chairman, "is good. The evidence that he is in Liverpool is less good. A telegram is not necessarily despatched by the man whose name is signed to it. Further, it seems to me improbable that a young bachelor would have been selected for the high office which Mr. Hesseltine claims to have fulfilled. I think we shall do better than that. I will ask Mr. Pusely-Smythe how far he has succeeded in being in two places at once."

"It is easier to be in one place at twice," said Pusely-Smythe. "But I have done what I could, considering how unversed I am in the arts of deception." The applause which greeted this statement was possibly of an ironical character. "On the morning of Tuesday last," Pusely-Smythe continued, "I was at the Rectory, Meldon Bois, where I had been spending the week-end. The village of Meldon Bois is one hundred and eight miles from London. It had been my intention to leave Meldon Bois by the 10.5 a.m. for London. I had been pressed to remain for one more night, as there was to be a performance of a pastoral play by distinguished amateurs in the grounds of the Rectory on Tuesday afternoon, and it would be a pity for me to miss it. I will not conceal it from you, sir, that the said pastoral play constituted the principal reason for my departure.

"You have grasped these facts? Very good. Now, on the morning of Tuesday, by the first post, I received a letter from my one and only aunt, who resides in London, to say that as I was coming up to town that morning she hoped I would lunch with her in Grosvenor Street and accompany her afterwards to hear a lecture to be given by some eminent idiot on 'The Future of Eugenics.' My aunt is one of the most strong-minded and wearisome women in existence. I had been reluctant to witness the amateur performance in the Rectory grounds, and I contemplated the idea of listening to a lecture on 'The Future of Eugenics' with horror and loathing. That was the situation. I had to miss two birds with one stone.

"My first step was to telegraph to my one and only aunt as follows: 'Regret detained here. Am writing.' On the following morning she received a letter from me which I am able to produce in its envelope. The letter is in my own handwriting on paper stamped with the Rectory address. The letter is dated Tuesday evening, and the post-mark on the envelope shows that it was posted at Meldon Bois on that day. Now that letter not only states that I had remained so as not to miss the pastoral amateurs, but also makes several statements as to their performance, every one of which can be proved to be absolutely accurate. These statements are that Miss Sykes looked charming in some pale lilac-coloured contraption, that the comedian overacted, that the weather was not entirely favourable, that some of the players seemed to find a difficulty in making themselves audible, that quite a nice sum was realised for the Cottage Hospital, and that the Rector in proposing a vote of thanks to the players said that where all were so good it would be invidious to differentiate. I have no doubt that on the strength of that letter and the details it contains, my aunt would give evidence in good faith that to her knowledge I must have been at Meldon Bois on Tuesday afternoon. Notwithstanding this, I left Meldon Bois on Tuesday morning by the train originally contemplated, and on Tuesday afternoon I was playing bridge at my club in London, as various members of the club who met me there would attest."

"On the face of it," said the chairman, "it looks like rather a good case. I presume that you wrote the letter to your aunt before leaving by train in the morning, and gave it to a servant with instructions to post it after the performance."

"Precisely so."

"But how did you manage to give an accurate account of the performance at which you were really not present?"

"Well, Miss Sykes was staying at the Rectory and had told me what dress she would wear. The rest was intelligent anticipation. The glass was low, and, besides, the weather is always unfavourable for pastoral plays, and some of the players always fail to make their voices carry in the open. Given village amateurs, over-acting by the comedian is as certain as death. To put the receipts as a nice sum was quite safe. It was riskier to quote the Rector's actual words, but he's a kindly and tactful man with a circumscribed mind, so I thought I might chance it, and it came off."

The next few members on whom the chairman called produced nothing of interest. Some, like Hesseltine, had thought of the bogus telegram. Some, like Feldane, were resting. Dr. Alden had tried an idea of his own, and expressed the hope that the chairman would think better of it than he did himself.

Early one morning he had entered a tobacconist's shop where he was not known and investigated the man's stock of cigars. He found it difficult to make up his mind as to which of three different brands would suit him best. He took away with him a specimen of each, and said that he would try them after luncheon and let the tobacconist know. At three that afternoon Dr. Alden's man called at the tobacconist's with a note from the doctor saying that the trial had been made and naming the brand selected. Five hundred of this brand were ordered, and a cheque for the exact sum was enclosed in payment. The tobacconist was to deliver the goods to the bearer of the note, as the doctor was leaving for the country at four and wished to take some of the cigars with him. This was done, and probably the tobacconist would have been willing to swear in consequence that Dr. Alden was in London until four that day. As a matter of fact, the doctor had left for the North by express shortly after ten that morning.

"Yes," said the chairman, "you convinced that tobacconist that you were in London when you were not, just as Pusely-Smythe convinced his aunt that he was not in London when he was. In each case it is the evidence of one person only. Have you done any better, Mr. Wildersley?"

"Better?" said Wildersley cheerfully. "I should rather think I have. I should have made out the club cheque for the prize to my own order already but for the fact that I prefer the formal routine. Cast your chairmaniacal eye over this sketch-book. It is filled with pencil drawings made from time to time, if not oftener, by the eminent Wildersley. The last few pages were made at the political meeting at Glasgow last week. They are dated in my own hand. There are notes as to the colour also in my hand. They are in my sketch-book. If they are not proof positive that I was at that meeting, then what are they? All the same I was in London while that meeting was being held, and can produce countless witnesses who saw me and spoke to me."

The chairman looked carefully at the drawings. "Not done from photographs, I suppose?"

"No, m'lord," said Wildersley. "All genuine hand-work and done on the spot."

Lord Herngill compared them with previous drawings in the book. "These look to me," he said, "as if they were done by somebody who was trying to imitate your technique but had not quite got it."

"Yes," said Wildersley, "that finishes us. You have it. The other artist member and I went into collaboration in this enterprise. Austin went to Glasgow, and made the sketches in the book with what he was pleased to call an imitation of the worst of the Wildersleian mannerisms. I remained in London giving my famous impersonation of myself. I added the date and manuscript notes afterwards. Still, if this book fell into the hands of somebody who had not the full use of his eyes —and very few people have—he might use it as evidence in good faith that I was at Glasgow at that date."

"Undoubtedly. I shall not forget your claim. Meanwhile, is there any other?"

"Yes," said Sir Charles Bunford placidly, "I think my claim to have established an alibi is stronger than any you have heard yet. Birmingham is more than a hundred miles from London. A certain butler in Birmingham would swear that he saw me and spoke to me on a certain afternoon. A photographer in Birmingham would swear that he photographed me on that same afternoon, and would be able to produce the negative. Yet during the whole of that afternoon I was in London, as the evidence of many of my friends would show. And all the evidence would be given in good faith."

"And how was this miracle accomplished?" the chairman asked.

"I'll tell you the story as briefly as I can. I went to stay for a fortnight with an old friend of mine, a bachelor named Fraser, who has a house outside Birmingham. He is a keen ornithologist. He employs in the preparation of specimens and so on a curious character called Mitten, who is just as keen on birds as Fraser himself. Fraser only has Mitten's spare time. Mitten's regular work is with a Birmingham photographer, for whom he does developing and also has charge of the stock of negatives. Fraser is quite unlike me in the face, except that we both have the same deficiency of colour in the hair, but we are of about the same height and build. There is also a slight similarity in our voices. That was the rough material that I had at my disposal, and no doubt you can guess how I got my results from it."

"You'd better continue," said the chairman, smiling.

"On the day before I left I pointed out to Fraser that a similarity in mass often prevented a dissimilarity in detail from being noticed, and that the attitude of expectant attention is a frequent source of error. Fraser asked me, as I had thought he would, what I meant and what I was getting at. I replied that by taking advantage of two facts I had mentioned he could probably get himself mistaken for me. He said that nobody would make the mistake. I said that Hammond's butler would make it on the following afternoon, if he cared to try the experiment.

"'I'd like to try it, but it's impossible. That butler has known me for the last two years, and he has only seen you four or five times in the afternoon. How could he be taken in?'

"'He has always seen you in dark and chastened clothing, such as it is your custom to wear. He has always seen me with a gray bowler, a light suit, white spats, and a distinctive necktie. He expects to see me tomorrow afternoon, because I borrowed an umbrella there to-day, and said I would bring it back then. All you have to do is to wear my clothes, and hand in that umbrella. He will expect to see me. He will actually see my clothes on a man of about my figure. The hall at the Hammonds' house is rather dark, and you will have the sun behind you. It's quite certain the man will be mistaken.'

"It was tried and happened as I had foretold. The butler addressed Fraser as Sir Charles."

"But how did you manage about the photograph?"

"That was done by means of a bet. Old Mitten is a great believer in system, and has his own infallible method for cataloguing photographic negatives so that a mistake is impossible. I chaffed him about it and told him that I would cause him to enter two lots of negatives wrongly. I offered to bet a sovereign on it and he accepted with avidity. I then settled with Fraser what we would do. Fraser booked an appointment with the photographer for the morning that I left for London, and I booked another for myself in the afternoon, the appointments being made by post. I kept Fraser's appointment just before I left for the station, and Fraser kept mine in the afternoon after he had finished with Hammond's butler. Mitten found out what had been done, of course, catalogued the negatives correctly, and has collected his sovereign. But I understand that he has not informed his employer, on the ground that the employer dislikes larks. The entries in the appointment book remain as they were. So that it is on record that I was photographed in the afternoon, though the photographic negatives entered under my name are really those taken from me in the morning."

"This," said the chairman, "is the most elaborate attempt we have had. Nobody else claims to have been seen in two places at the same time. I do not say that the evidence is perfect, but then the evidence of an alibi must always have a hole in it somewhere. Does anybody claim to have beaten it? Nobody? Then I have no hesitation in deciding in Sir Charles's favour, and I congratulate him on the distinction—which, so far, has been held by Mr. Pusely-Smythe alone—of winning the prize on two successive occasions."

The next problem was now read out. It was entitled "The Threepenny Problem," and ran as follows: "It is required to offer a halfcrown for a threepenny bus-fare, and to receive the change wholly in threepenny bits. No gift or promise of a gift may be made to the conductor to induce him to give the change in this form."

"That's the easiest we've ever had," grumbled Major Byles. "So, of course, it's my turn to be in the chair, and I can't compete."

No. X
The Threepenny Problem

"Child's-play," said Major Byles, "that's what this problem is. It is required to offer a half-crown for a threepenny bus-fare, and to receive the change wholly in threepenny-bits. And you're not allowed to give the conductor anything or promise him anything as an inducement to let you have the nine threepennies. It's my belief that you'd only have to ask in a civil way, and any conductor would do it for you. A more obliging set of men than the London bus-conductors couldn't be found, except, perhaps, the London police. I don't call it a problem at all. You'll all win, of course, and that will mean a comfortable tenner for every member of the club except myself— just because I'm stuck up here in the chair. It's scandalous." He snipped the end of a cigar ferociously, and lit it as if he took pleasure in its destruction—which, indeed, may have been the case. "However, I must do my duty, and I'll call on my reverend friend, Mr. Cunliffe, to tell us what he has done about it."

"My story is a sad one," said the Rev. Septimus Cunliffe. "It leads me to believe that our chairman has over-estimated the amiability of the conductors and underestimated the difficulty of the problem. I gave a half-crown for a threepenny fare, and told the man that it would be a great kindness if he could let me have my change in threepenny pieces. He never said a word, but handed me a florin and three coppers.

"'Did you hear what I asked you?' I said to him.

"'Oh, yes,' he said, 'I heard. If you want all them threepennies, you'd better get them out of the blanky offertory-bag next Sunday!'"

"Extraordinary," said the chairman. "Something must have occurred to ruffle the man's temper. Did you find any difficulty, Bunford?"

"I failed absolutely," said Sir Charles Bunford. "No doubt I made a mistake in putting my request during the busy hour of the morning. The conductor looked resigned but sardonic.

"'Want it all in threepennies, do you?' he said. 'Would you like them of any particular year?'

"I said that the date was immaterial. Any year would do.

"'That's all right,' he said. 'Then you can wait for next year's.' And he gave me a shilling, a sixpence, and ninepence in what is generally described at the inquest as bronze."

"Of course," said the chairman, "it was a mistake to bother the man when he was busy. And a little tact is wanted. If I'd been in for this competition myself I shouldn't just have asked for my change in threepennies, I should have given some plausible reason for wanting it."

"With great respect, sir," said Mr. Quillian, "I must differ from you. I had the same idea and tried it. I told the conductor that I had a bet that I would get my change entirely in threepennies. I thought it would appeal to his sporting instinct. All he said was, 'You've lost, then,' and gave me the change without as much as one threepenny in it. Seemed rather pleased about it, too."

"I'd much the same experience," said Dr. Alden. "As I gave the man my half-crown I mentioned that I was a collector of threepenny bits, and asked him if he could help me. He gave me two shillings and three pennies.

"'Well,' he said, 'if you like to step off at the Bank of England and ask the Chief Cashier to give you threepennies for that little lot, you can mention my name.'"

"It's quite possible," said the chairman, "that those conductors had not got the threepennies to give you. I go for days sometimes without as much as seeing a threepenny bit. It really looks as if the problem presented more difficulties than I had at first supposed. Did you manage to surmount them, Mr. Matthews?"

"Can't say I did, though I took a lot of trouble about it. There's no two ways about it—if you put an unreasonable request to a complete stranger, whether he's a bus-conductor or anything else, you're likely to be sat on and not to get what you want either. I picked a bus in the slack time, running nearly empty, with a good-natured-looking conductor. I chatted with him for five minutes, and got him friendly disposed towards me, before I even mentioned threepennies. Then I asked him if he got many of them. He said he took enough of them to fill a pint-pot some days and he wished he didn't. They were finicky things to handle and easy dropped. Well, that was a very good start. I gave him a half-crown for my three-penny ticket and told him that I would be glad to take as many threepenny bits off his hands as he liked to give me. Said I wanted them for a young nephew of mine. The man was quite willing, and if anybody had offered me twenty pounds just then for my chance of winning the prize to-night I'd have refused it. If anybody would give me twenty pence for the same chance at the present moment I'd jump at it. The trouble came in just as the chairman has indicated. The man looked through his silver and did his best for me, but one solitary threepenny was all he could raise. I got that one, of course, but one is not nine. It was just rotten bad luck. He said that nineteen days in twenty he could have given me a dozen of them, but he supposed it had to happen so."

"You call that bad luck?" said the Hon. James Feldane gloomily. "Not half as bitter as mine."

"We'll have the story of your failure, Jimmy," said the chairman.

"Failure's nothing. I've failed before and shall do again. It's what happened afterwards that worries me. All the same, I don't know that I should have failed if I had simply trusted to my own judgment, but the woman looked so smart and brainy that I let myself be influenced, though she was really talking clotted nonsense."

"You're getting on too quickly," said the chairman. "To what woman do you refer?"

"How should I know? I haven't an idea what her name is. She was one of a pack of hens that I found cackling in my sister's drawing-room. They were discussing their maids and how to manage them, same as women have always done since the year one. The brainy-looking one said that when she had a reasonable order to give a maid, she always put it in the form of a request; but if she had an unreasonable request to make to a maid, she always put it in the form of an order. She said that this always bluffed the maid out. I thought there might be something in that bit of wisdom. If you give an order in an ordinary way, as if it were a matter of course, it may get taken in that spirit. Anyway, I thought I'd try it with the bus-conductor. I gave him my halfcrown, and said in my light and casual way. 'Threepenny ticket. And give me my change in three-penny bits.'

"He didn't say anything. He just glared at me. If he had said anything it would probably have scorched the top off the bus. He gave me my change—with never a threepenny bit in it—and then glared some more. He'd got rather a good glare. Broke up my nerves, anyhow. At the next corner I hopped off.

"Now mark the sequel. A little later I owed a taxi eightpence, gave the man a halfcrown and waited for my change. 'Sorry, sir,' said the man, 'but I shall have to give you six threepenny bits. I've got no other silver.'

"And that's the way things happen. When you want a thing you can't get it, and when you don't want it it's chucked at you."

"Well, really," said the chairman, without a blush, "as I fore-saw, this turns out to be a very difficult problem. No interruptions, please. I know that I did not actually say that it was very difficult, but it was in my mind. It looked easy, as I pointed out in my open-ing remarks, but nobody knows better than I do that appearances are often deceptive. I shall call upon our great expert and prize-winner, Mr. Pusely-Smythe. I am confident that he will have realised the difficulties and taken his measures accordingly."

Mr. Pusely-Smythe smiled grimly and sardonically. "Thank you, sir," he said, "for your kind words. I do not want to brag, but I gave this problem my very earnest consideration, and I do think that I realised some at least of the difficulties before me. I saw, firstly, that it was possible and even probable that the conductor might not have nine threepenny-bits to give me. Now some company-promoters have found out that the best way to get gold out of a gold-mine is to start by putting a little gold into it. I adopted that principle. I selected a certain bus on a certain route. I arranged that on the journey just before I made my appearance no fewer than twelve passengers would pay their fares with threepenny-bits. It only required a little organisation. If you tell a human boy or even a human girl to take your threepenny bit, pay a penny bus fare with it, and keep the change, you get willing service without any troublesome demand for explanations. Secondly, I had to have a story to tell the conductor that would induce him to oblige me. I was prepared to tell him that a friend had promised me that if I could collect a thousand threepenny-bits for the London Hospital, he would add double that amount to it.

"I notice, sir, an unworthy expression of suspicion on the face of my learned friend Mr. Quillian. My story for the conductor was not only plausible—it was actually true. I was the man who had made that promise to myself. (If I am not my own friend, who is?) Further, I was so absolutely certain of success that I remitted the sum in question, thirty-two pounds ten shillings, to the hospital and have a receipt for it. When I deducted the thirty-two pounds ten shillings expenditure from the hundred and ten pounds prize, I calculated that it would still leave a living wage for myself. Well, that was the position. I saw that there were two main difficulties in this problem, and I had arranged to meet both of them."

"Quite so," said the chairman. "As I've always said, these things need to be worked out in a clear-minded and systematic way. And the result was all right?"

Pusely-Smythe's smile was more sardonic than ever. "Much depends on the point of view; it was all right from some points of view. Punctually at the time I had fixed I took my seat on the top of the bus I had selected. About a minute later the conductor came up to collect the fares. I felt for my half-crown. I had not got any half-crown. I had no money on me whatever. I had inadvertently left my money at home. There was nobody on the bus to whom I could apply for temporary assistance. Well, there was no help for it. The conductor was weary, but firm. He told me to hop off the bus and not to try it on again. I hopped. It may have been all right from the point of view of the other competitors, but from my own point of view it was less satisfactory. And it only shows, as we all know, that you may lose your game by missing a perfectly easy shot."

Mr. Wildersley, A.R.A., had demanded threepennies from a conductor on the ground that he was collecting them. The conductor had replied that he was there to take the fares, not to supply private museums. Mr. Austin had met a most obliging conductor, who, however, had no threepennies in his possession. Lord Herngill and Mr. Hesseltine had only contemptuous refusals to record.

This, of course, happened before the war. In times when the gentler, kindlier, and more refined sex has charge of our public vehicles, the problem might prove easy of solution.

"Well," the chairman began, "it looks as if the whole lot of you duffers had failed." Here the secretary, Lord Herngill, whispered a few warning words in his ear, and the chairman nodded assent.

"Yes," he resumed, "it may look to you duffers as if the whole lot of you had failed, but of course that would be wrong. Nobody has succeeded in getting nine threepennies in change. But in that case the nearest approximation to that number wins. Mr. Matthews got one threepenny, and conformed to the conditions. Nobody else even got one. Therefore I declare Mr. Matthews to be the winner, and the club cheque for one hundred and ten pounds will be drawn to his order."

Jimmy Feldane confided his private sorrows to his friend Hesseltine. "I don't mind old Matthews winning. He's a genial old bird, and what he don't know about the noble art of dining ain't worth worrying over. But there is just one thing that makes me want to kick myself round and round this room till I get giddy. When Matthews told us his yarn, he said he'd take twenty pence for his chance of the prize. I ought to have been on to it in a flash, if not sooner. One-and-eight for a sporting chance of a hundred and ten pounds is good enough. The more I think of it, the more I see that I ought not to be allowed out except in charge of a nursemaid."

"Oh, we all missed that chance," said Hesseltine. "Maybe a little drink might do us some good."

While they were taking the medicine indicated, the chairman read out the problem which was to employ them during the following month. The fantastic editor of *The Pig-Keepers' Friend* had entitled it, "The Q-Loan Problem," and its terms were as follows:—

"It is required in three days to borrow as many things as possible, the name of each thing to begin with the letter Q. Nothing counts for the competition if its name is on the list of more than one member. No money may be given or promised in respect of any loan."

"And to-morrow morning, bright and early," said Jimmy, "I'm off to the Zoo in a taxi to see if I can't borrow their quagga."

No. XI
The Q-Loan Problem

The problem which came up for adjudication on this occasion was as follows:—

"It is required in three days to borrow as many things as possible, the name of each thing to begin with the letter Q. Nothing counts for the competition if its name is on the list of more than one member. No money may be given or promised in respect of any loan."

"I've arranged this," said Mr. Austin, who was the chairman for the evening, "so as to avoid any overstrain for myself. I shall call on that notorious painter and decorator, Mr. Wildersley, to begin with his list. When he has finished he will call on somebody else. The second man in his turn will name the third, and so on. If anything is read out by another member which is also down on your own list, hold up your hand. The secretary will keep the score. That leaves me absolutely nothing to do until it is time to announce the winner, and I shall probably go to sleep. So don't make any disturbing noises, please. You can begin now, Wildersley."

"My score is six," said Wildersley, "unless some of you selfish men have had the same ideas as I have. On my first day I borrowed two things—one of which people seem to show hesitation about lending, while the other was a thing that very few people have got to lend nowadays. In fact, I borrowed a quid and a quill-pen."

Many hands went up.

"This is painful and surprising," said Wildersley, "and reduces my score to four. On the second day I visited a female relative, said that I had a cold coming on, and had no difficulty in borrowing some quinine and a quilt."

But a show of hands indicated that others had found it equally easy.

"That brings me down to two, but the last two are good. I doubt if any other member could have thought of them, or could have borrowed them in any case. But I happen to know a painter who has got whole wardrobes full of costumes—uses them for his alleged pictures. From him I borrowed, firstly, a queue."

"I appeal to the chairman," said Jimmy Feldane confidently. "That word is spelled with a K."

"No," said the chairman. "You are probably thinking of the Gardens of the same name."

"In any case it's the thing they have outside the pit entrance, and you can't borrow it."

"That will be for Mr. Wildersley to explain."

"I did not borrow a crowd outside a pit entrance," said Wildersley. "But I did borrow the tie of a wig, which is another meaning of the word. That's one to me, anyhow. And I also borrowed a quoif."

"Surely, sir," said Mr. Quillian, "that word is spelled with a C?"

The chairman consulted a useful work of reference, and announced that the word was spelled in both ways.

"May we have your authority for that statement?"

"Standard dictionary."

"And will you define a standard dictionary for the purposes of this competition?"

"For the purposes of this competition a standard dictionary is any dictionary that was published subsequently to the eighteenth century and cost more than fivepence-halfpenny originally."

"It doesn't much matter really, for as the word is also on my own list neither Wildersley nor I can score it."

"You might have said that before," said the chairman. "It looks as if you were giving me trouble on purpose."

And it is quite possible that his surmise was correct. The Problem Club does not allow its chairman to sleep when on duty. Sir

Charles Bunford requested him to state what Mr. Wildersley's score was; and it may not have been from inadvertence that Wildersley neglected to name his successor and left it to the chairman to do so. He called upon Dr. Alden.

"Well," said the Doctor, "I had borrowed quinine, of course, but that has been ruled out. I also borrowed some quassia from the same man. No hands up? I think I score one for quassia, if the chairman admits it."

The chairman consulted his dictionary and said that quassia appeared to be all right. He was immediately asked by Mr. Pusely-Smythe if he could inform the members whether quassia was a summer drink or an intermittent fever.

"At the present moment," said Mr. Austin severely, "I am giving my most eager and concentrated attention to the conscientious discharge of my arduous duties. I cannot be interrupted by purely frivolous questions. Dr. Alden will proceed."

"I further borrowed a quadrant and a thermometer."

"I fear," said the chairman, "that I must rule that the word thermometer does not begin with the letter Q."

"Your rapid grasp of these fine points, sir, impels my admiration. But with great respect I would point out that this thermometer contained mercury, and therefore in borrowing the thermometer I borrowed quicksilver. My remaining loans consisted of a quarto and a quotation."

But other members had borrowed both a quarto and a quotation. Dr. Alden was accordingly left with a score of three.

Major Byles, who came next, had done better. In the course of a morning stroll with a neighbouring landowner over his property, he had borrowed some weird things. His list consisted of a quarry, a quicksand, some quickset, quitch-grass, and quick-lime. And as none of these things had been borrowed by any other member he scored five. But he did not seem entirely happy about it.

"The trouble with these problems," he said, "is that one has to do absolutely idiotic things, and consequently one is likely to be thought an absolute idiot. I did the best I could. I invented quite a plausible story about a geological friend to account for the quarry and the quicksand. But I believe that my neighbour goes about saying that poor old Byles is far from well, and tapping his forehead to indicate the nature of my complaint. It's most unpleasant. Still, five ain't such a bad score. How did you get on with that quagga, Jimmy?"

"Nothing doing," said Jimmy. "I went to the Zoo, just as I said I would. But, if you ask me, the whole place is rotten with red tape and officialism. They wouldn't lend me the blessed quagga, though I promised them I'd return it in five minutes. Said it was not customary to lend out the animals, and a lot of silly talk like that. Quite obstinate about it, too. I'd got Hesseltine there to take a snapshot of me shepherding the quagga in the wilds of Regent's Park, and it simply meant our valuable time thrown away. Also, it appeared that quaggas are out of print and they'd not got one.

"But quite apart from that I'm not claiming to have won. I've only got two things down on my list that have not been claimed so far. The first was the queen of spades from a pack of cards, and the second is the four kings from the same pack. I don't spell the word king with a Q, but the four of them are a quatorse, at piquet. But a score of two's no use, and I shall probably be described on my tombstone as brainy but unfortunate. Meanwhile I notice a sunny smile on the face of our padre, as if he were a prize-winner. He might tell us how he did it."

The Rev. Septimus Cunliffe had certainly been energetic and industrious. To start with he had called upon an old friend of his, a man of some learning, with an interest in music and a fair library. Here he had no difficulty in borrowing Quixote, Quivedo, Quintillian, Quain, and some quadrilles, quartets, and quintets. He engaged his host in a discussion as to the precise meaning of a quip, a quirk, and a quiddity, persuaded him to write down an instance of each, and borrowed the instances. He borrowed a quatrain of his host's composition, and twenty-four sheets of notepaper, which make a quire.

The next two days were less productive, but he borrowed a specimen of quartz from one man, and a dog, which was unquestionably a quadruped, from another. A lady who was interested in archery lent him a quiver. Loans of a quoit, a quart of milk, and a quarter of coal were also negotiated.

But all the same, his smile of self-congratulation was premature. He was not destined to score eighteen, for the simple reason that he had not borrowed a single thing which was not on the list of either Lord Herngill, or Mr. Quillian, or Mr. Pusely-Smythe. And they in their turn could not score because everything on their lists was also on the parson's. Industry had cancelled industry; ingenuity had destroyed ingenuity.

The only other member who could produce a score at all was Mr. Matthews. He registered a modest score of one for having borrowed a quarrel. It was in vain that Hesseltine maintained that you could pick a quarrel but could not borrow one. The chairman referred to his standard dictionary and learned that a quarrel was not necessarily a dispute; it might be a diamond-shaped pane of glass, which was, in fact, what Mr. Matthews had borrowed.

"Well," said the chairman, "Major Byles is the winner, and I think he deserves to be. The rest of you were a tame set of sheep, laborious and ingenious, but without any proper spirit of enterprise. But nobody could walk out calmly one morning and borrow a quarry and a quicksand unless he were really adventurous. To do that was magnificent and Elizabethan. I confess that I should like to know what the neighbour said when the Major borrowed the quitch-grass."

"Oh, the old chap didn't say much," said Major Byles. "That was the last thing I borrowed, and by that time he seemed rather worried and nervous. I told him quite a good story, too, about a nephew in London who wanted a specimen for botanical purposes. The real trouble was that, as it had to be a loan, I sent the beastly weed back to him three days later. That was when he decided I really must have had a touch of the sun, or had given way to the habit, or something of that kind. But I shall live it down. Anyway, I've won, and I don't care if it snows."

"Quite so. In the problems of this club, as in the problems of life, it sometimes happens that courage and character will do more than low cunning to effect a solution. And I hope that this will be a lesson to certain members who, by a series of vexatious and need-less questions, have deprived me of my proper rest this evening. However, I shall shortly be taking it out of them at bridge, and they have my forgiveness."

"If," said Pusely-Smythe, "the chairman has finished infring-ing the prerogative of our padre by delivering a sermon, he will perhaps inform us what the next problem is."

"Certainly," said the chairman cheerfully. "I was forgetting. It is Dr. Alden's turn to take the chair next time, but complications have arisen. I've had a letter from the talented editor of *The Pig-Keeper's Friend*, who sets our problems, and, as you will remem-ber, was introduced to us by Lord Herngill. It appears that, in con-sequence of his personal knowledge of the esteemed editor, Lord Herngill would have an unfair advantage in this next competition, and is therefore with his own consent disqualified for it. But for the same reason he is specially qualified to adjudicate on the prob-lem. I have mentioned the matter to Herngill and the Doctor, and they are both willing to exchange their turns as chairman. So that, subject to your approval, Herngill will be the chairman at our next meeting. I will put it to you, gentlemen."

The proposal met with general approval.

"That's all right," said the chairman. "Then we can have the card-tables brought in. And if I can only manage to cut with the Major, I fancy that our opponents will have a pretty thin time. This is his evening."

"I do not wish," said Mr. Quillian solemnly, "to dispute the statement, but even now we do not know what the problem for next month is to be."

"You're right," said the chairman; "you're absolutely right. It's funny, but if I forget a thing once I nearly always forget it twice. However, as a matter of fact, I don't yet know it myself. Here it is in its sealed envelope. We will investigate it."

He tore open the envelope and glanced at the contents.

"Well," he said, "I really don't know why he made so much fuss about it. You couldn't have anything simpler. He calls it 'The Pig-Keeper's Problem.' This is all it is: 'It is required to buy a copy of

the current issue of *The Pig-Keepers' Friend*.' I don't see any difficulty about that, do you, Leonard?"

But Leonard declined to be drawn. "I should like to have notice of that question," he said.

No. XII
The Pig-Keeper's Problem

"Well, gentlemen," said the chairman, Lord Herngill, "you have been required to purchase a copy of the current issue of *The Pig-Keepers' Friend*. It is generally published on the seventh of every month, but if the talented editor happens to be thinking about something else at the time—as occasionally happens—it may come out a few days later. It is published according to the law, but it cannot be said to court circulation. It is exposed for sale in certain places, but I doubt if any copy has been purchased by the general public for the last year—at any rate, not until the members of this club went on the hunt for it. How did you get on, Major Byles?"

"Wish I'd never gone in for it," snapped the Major. "I told my regular newsagent to get me a copy. He said he hadn't heard of it, but would make inquiries. At the end of a week he came to me with a story that, as far as he had been able to learn, the paper had discontinued publication a year before. I knew that was a lie, of course, and told him so, and said I'd finished with him. There's only one other newsagent near me, and I had to go to him. His beastly boy leaves the wrong papers at the house every morning, and seems to think I'm a Socialist like himself. The end of it will be that I shall have to eat my own words and go back to the other man. Destroys all discipline, that kind of thing."

Dr. Alden, Pusely-Smythe, and several others had hunted trade lists and directories in vain. Mr. Matthews had lavished money on advertisements, offering a sovereign for a copy of the current issue of *The Pig-Keepers' Friend*, and had received no reply.

Sir Charles Bunford had written to an old friend who held a
high position at the British Museum, asking him to get hold of some
recent number of *The Pig-Keepers' Friend*, and let him have the
address at which it was published. After some delay the friend replied that he had seen a copy of the periodical, and that it appeared
to be the work of a lunatic, and that the address given in it was
"The Impersonation Society, Boswell Court, Fleet Street."

"It certainly looked to me," said Sir Charles, "as if I had got
hold of the right end of the stick. I found the office, which appeared
to occupy the whole of the top floor of the building. The name of
the society was painted on the outer door, and underneath was the
legend, 'Hours, Ten to Four.' It was then eleven in the morning. I
knocked and rang, and could get no answer at all, and I could hear
no sound of any activity within. I came back at three in the afternoon with the same result. I then sent a letter, saying that I required a copy of the current number of the paper, and wished to
know what amount I should forward for the purpose; and to make
it quite certain I enclosed a stamped and addressed envelope. Well,
I got a reply, with an illegible signature. It said that no retail business was done at the office, but that I could apply for the copy
through the usual channels. I still thought that I was on the right
line, and gave the address to my newsagent and set him to work.
The answer he got was that the current issue was out of print, all
copies having been allocated. So there I stuck."

"You came rather near to it, though," said the chairman. "Suppose we shorten matters. Does any member claim to have won this
competition? Our friend Jimmy has been looking rather pleased
with himself all the evening."

"Have I?" said Jimmy. "Well, I don't mind admitting that I've
jolly good reason to be pleased with myself just now, quite apart
from the competition. I've won that too, as it happens. But I don't
take much credit for it. Of course, you could say that it was due to
the improved habits and all that, and I suppose that was so, more
or less, but the fact remains that I wasn't even thinking about the
thing at the time, and if I hadn't forgotten my cigarette-case it

would never have happened. So if you don't call it luck, what are you to call it?"

"Mr. Feldane," said the chairman, with great gravity, "you are beginning your story at the wrong end—that is, with the criticism of it. I must ask you to tell us simply what happened from the very commencement, and as coherently as possible."

"Certainly," said Jimmy indulgently, "any old way that you happen to fancy. Well, to start with, though as a matter of fact it had been going on for more than a week before, they asked me to dine with them at the house on Wimbledon Common. So naturally I jumped at it. I won't say I had always been addicted to the scenery of Wimbledon, but there were certain private reasons."

"Private reasons for dining at Wimbledon?" said Hesseltine reflectively. "I think I know her name, don't I?"

"Wish you wouldn't interrupt just at the moment when I'm being coherent. I was going to dine at Wimbledon, and it takes some doing to get there. My own little car was in hospital, and the natural way seemed to be to take a taxi, and let it tick up the twopences until I wanted to go back. Then I reflected that I had decided to give up all silly extravagance, and on inquiry I found that there was a place called Waterloo Station from which I could book to Wimbledon. So I did so. I didn't smoke on my way out, which must have been a kind of absentmindedness. It was on my way back that I found that I had forgotten my cigarette-case. Now nothing makes you feel you must smoke so much as the knowledge that you can't. I hopped out at Vauxhall and found a taxi right away—I'd got all the luck in the world that night. I told the driver where to go and to stop at a tobacconist's, and do it soon. The shop he stopped at, in a back street off a side street, didn't look up to much, but I was desperate and ready to smoke anything that was called a Turkish cigarette. Behind the counter I found a fat, middle-aged man reading a book. He gave me something that would do, took my money, and called me sir. But he was no more a tobacconist than I am.

"Tobacconists may do a lot of funny things, but they don't read the *Agamemnon* of Æschylus in the original Greek, which is what this blighter was doing. Nor do they have manicured nails and an Oxford intonation—his attempt at a Cockney accent was one of the most pathetic failures I've ever met. However, that's not the point. The point is that on the counter was a small pile of copies of the current number of *The Pig-Keepers' Friend*. The number consisted of sixteen pages, and they were very small pages, and the price was one pound, but I did not hesitate. I bought my copy, and I have it in my pocket now. I'll hand it up to our chairman. I've had a glance at it myself, and I'm inclined to agree with that Museum Johnnie. It's got nothing to do with pigs. It's mostly poetry and the rest is foolishness. It beats me altogether."

The chairman examined the copy of the paper which had been handed to him. "There is no doubt about it," he said. "This is a copy of the current issue, and Mr. Feldane assures us that he bought it. No other claim is put forward. The club's cheque for one hundred and ten pounds will therefore be drawn to the order of Mr. Feldane. Has any member anything to add?"

"I have," said Mr. Matthews. "The whole thing wants clearing up, and I hope our chairman will clear it. Is our problem-setter really a lunatic? What is he doing with this weird paper of his? What's the Impersonation Society? Who was the over-educated tobacconist? We'd like the whole story."

And to this there was general assent.

"I've no objection," said Lord Herngill. "Willy Bunting has empowered me to tell you anything I like about him, including the truth. The fact is that in this problem the members of this club have come up against another organisation, the Impersonation Society, which is one of Bunting's curious inventions.

"I first knew him as an undergraduate. I thought a good deal of his ability both as a poet and as an amateur actor. He was also no end of a lark. He was not a lunatic, but he had endless eccentricities. He had no ambitions, a contempt for public opinion, and a determination to do just as he liked. He was sent down for impersonating one of the proctors. He was beautifully made up, and looked exactly like that proctor, but he had the misfortune to meet the original in Trumpington Street.

"This disaster did not greatly trouble him. He had more money than was good for him and was not intending to take up any profession. He came to London, and shortly afterwards he started the Impersonation Society. His theory was that the ordinary holiday is a mistake, and that what a tired man or woman wants is not only a change of place but a change of personality. In order to get a complete rest you must, for the time being, be somebody else. You must dress and live like the character you have assumed and you must even try to think like him. I am by no means sure that there is not something to be said for the idea. There must be plenty of people who think so, for the membership of the society has increased every year, and includes some of the very last people that you would expect to find in such an organisation.

"For instance, the man that Jimmy found in the tobacconist's shop in the Vauxhall neighbourhood, is in reality the head master and proprietor of a large and successful private school. All through term-time he is treated with intense respect. Little boys call him sir, and tremble before him. His assistant masters treat him with a deference which they are probably very far from feeling. He lives in an atmosphere of sickening and insincere flattery, and smoking is strictly prohibited. So in his holiday he becomes a tobacconist's assistant, smokes all day, goes about in his shirt-sleeves, treats customers with respect, is respected by nobody himself, professes no more virtues than he really has, and thoroughly enjoys it. He says that it keeps him sane. The shop itself is, of course, the property of the society, and a resident manager trains those members who wish to take a holiday there.

"I should perhaps explain why Sir Charles Bunford was unable to obtain entrance to the rooms of the society. He misinterpreted the legend on the door. The hours are ten to four, but they are from ten at night to four in the morning. I may add that it was once raided by the police, to the intense disappointment of the police and to the great joy of the members, particularly Willy Bunting.

"But I must tell you something of *The Pig-Keepers' Friend*. Willy's nearest relative is an irascible uncle, who told him that he was wasting his life. Willy said that, on the contrary, he was enjoying it. The uncle maintained that Willy did nothing, and Willy replied that he wrote poetry. Then the indignant uncle did a foolish thing. He said that he was prepared to bet a hundred pounds that Willy never had a poem accepted by the editor of any existing periodical published in London. Willy jumped at that bet. That moribund monthly, *The Pig-Keepers' Friend*, was at that time in the market. It had lost its circulation and had never had advertisements. The wretched enthusiast who had brought it into being was heartily sick of it. Willy offered a fiver for it, which was more than it was worth, and instantly became the proprietor. He then appointed himself editor, and in his editorial capacity accepted one of his own poems and printed it in the next issue. A prefatory note said that the editor had no doubt that the weary pig-keeper would be glad to beguile his hours of leisure with the following poem by his esteemed contributor, William Bunting. Willy sent a copy of it to his uncle, received his hundred, and was cut out of the uncle's last will and testament.

"Having acquired the magazine, Willy proceeded to make it the organ of the Impersonation Society. He still printed his own poems in it, and occasionally mine, but it was principally devoted to the cryptic record of the many strange activities of the Impersonation Society. The original title was retained, and occasional references to pigs and pig-keeping will be found in it. For instance, in the current number there are a number of spoof inquiries from agonised pig-keepers seeking the expert advice of the editor in their difficulties. One of them asks how, in the event of his pigs swarming, he is to know which of them is the queen. The editor's replies are humorous and in some cases, I regret to say, Rabelaisian.

"The present issue of the paper was on sale at the tobacconist's. It has also been offered in the public streets by a supposed newsvendor every day for the last month. The only copy purchased was bought by Jimmy, who found it by accident. As the paper is sold only by members, Mr. Matthews will understand why his advertisements failed to get any result. And now that I've answered your questions, I'd like to put one to our prize-winner."

"Go ahead," said Jimmy.

"How many times have you dined at Wimbledon in the last week?"

"Four times, as it happens. You see, the views there over the Common are really—"

"You needn't continue. You've said enough. I am sure that I may offer you the hearty congratulations of the club on your engagement."

"Well, I'm blest," said Jimmy. "I am engaged, I'm pleased and proud to say, but how on earth did you know?"

"In many ways, and I'll tell you one. Only one thing on earth could have made you forget your cigarette-case."

And naturally the next thing to do was to drink to the health of Jimmy and his future bride. And it was done with great enthusiasm.

And here the chronicles of the Problem Club must come to an end. The story of how Willy Bunting became a member of the club and subsequently retired from it, and how the solution of one problem brought the Rev. Septimus Cunliffe into the police-court, and how the solution of another made Mr. Matthews miss his dinner, and how a negro failed to get into the club, and how a girl of seventeen was actually elected—these things with many others must remain hidden in the club archives.

COACHWHIP PUBLICATIONS
COACHWHIPBOOKS.COM

THE COMPLETE ADVENTURES OF
ROMNEY PRINGLE

R. AUSTIN FREEMAN &
JOHN J. PITCAIRN
(AS BY CLIFFORD ASHDOWN)

COACHWHIP PUBLICATIONS
COACHWHIPBOOKS.COM

VULTURES
IN THE SKY
A HUGH RENNERT MYSTERY

TODD DOWNING

COACHWHIP PUBLICATIONS
COACHWHIPBOOKS.COM

THE CASEBOOK OF
MR. CARRINGTON
SIMON
CARRINGTON'S CASES
J. STORER CLOUSTON

COACHWHIP PUBLICATIONS
COACHWHIPBOOKS.COM

CRIMINAL ROGUES 1

The Exploits of Danby Croker
R. Austin Freeman

A Prince of Swindlers
Guy Boothby

12 CASES FOR
MAX
CARRADOS

ERNEST BRAMAH

DETECTIVES

4

MISS MADELYN MACK
HUGH C. WEIR

VIOLET STRANGE
ANNA KATHARINE GREEN

MISS VAN SNOOP
CLARENCE ROOK

FLORENCE CUSACK
MEADE & EUSTACE

www.ingramcontent.com/pod-product-compliance
Lightning Source LLC
Chambersburg PA
CBHW021920170626
46807CB00007B/2911